The Teacup Griffin

Wellspring Chronicles: Book 1

Tesha Geddes

2025

Copyright

Copyright © 2025 Tesha Geddes

All rights reserved. No portion of this book may be reproduced in any form without permission from the publisher, except as permitted by U.S. copyright law. For permissions contact: tgeddeswrites@gmail.com

While Arizona is a real state within the United States, and Phoenix and Tucson are real cities, the places, businesses and institutions mentioned within are works of fiction, as is the town of Wellspring and the train and robust public transportation system.

All characters and scenes are fictional. Any resemblance to persons (living or dead) is coincidental.

Acknowledgements

A big thank you to my editor, Elena

Cover design by Tesha Geddes

Composite photo created with pictures from: Marek Wolak, Anton Matyukha, Юрий Белошкурский, Hendrik Bogaard, and Eric Philippe Isselée on Depositphotos

Dedication

To my wonderful husband, with many thanks for all his support and encouragement. And to my sister, and her fount of knowledge on certain topics.

Characters:

- Agent Briarthorn: elf, member of Dylan's SAID team
- Agent Brown: large cat shifter, member of Dylan's SAID team.
- Azalea: Lucas' older sister
- Birch Fernleaf: Lucas' dad, elf
- Brick: troll, member of Dylan's SAID team
- Briggs: goblin mechanic, male
- Canterbury: teacup griffin, Lucas' familiar
- Chloe: barista
- Chrys (Chrysocolla): teacup griffin, Miriam's familiar
- Dylan Blazewing: dragon shifter, SAID agent, Lucas' friend
- Hattie: goblin, female
- Hester Fernleaf: Lucas' mom, gnome
- Iris: Lucas' younger sister
- Jason Stone: griffin shifter, SAID agent, Lucas' friend
- Jonas: Lucas' younger brother
- Lucas: Professor, male, elf-gnome
- Melanie: woodland fae, Nolan's sister, keeper of Phil
- Mike: Miriam's neighbor
- Miriam: protagonist, female
- Nolan: woodland fae, Lucas' friend
- Ollie: One of Lucas' students, and front desk clerk at the conservatory
- Orchid: Lucas' youngest sister
- Phil: a phoenix, Melanie's familiar
- Sean: bear shifter, Lucas' friend
- Shelby: barista
- Tony: clerk at Familiar Feed
- Trevor: troll mechanic, male
- Violet: bookshop owner, human, female

Contents

Copyright iii
Acknowledgements iii
Dedication v
List of characters: vi
Contents vii
Chapter 1 1
Chapter 2 9
Chapter 3 21
Chapter 4 27
Chapter 5 33
Chapter 6 39
Chapter 7 47
Chapter 8 55
Chapter 9 61
Chapter 10 65
Chapter 11 71
Chapter 12 77
Chapter 13 83
Chapter 14 89
Chapter 15 95
Chapter 16 103
Chapter 17 109
Chapter 18 117
Chapter 19 123
Chapter 20 131
Chapter 21 139
Chapter 22 147

Chapter 23	153
Chapter 24	159
Chapter 25	165
Chapter 26	171
Chapter 27	179
Chapter 28	185
Chapter 29	191
Chapter 30	197
Chapter 31	203
Chapter 32	211
Chapter 33	215
Chapter 34	219
Chapter 35	227
Chapter 36	231
Chapter 37	237
Chapter 38	243
Chapter 39	249
Chapter 40	255
Chapter 41	261
Chapter 42	269
Chapter 43	273
Chapter 44	279
Chapter 45	285
Epilogue	291
Afterword	295
About the Author	297
Other books by Tesha Geddes	299

Chapter 1

Miriam

WHO WRECKS A BOOKSTORE'S WINDOW DISPLAY?

I stared at the mess in front of me, trying to make sense of it. The weight of my late night hung heavy over my shoulders. I knew I should have gone to bed earlier, but I just *had* to finish that book. I'd rationalized it away, saying that today was going to be an easy day—the store was only open for a half-day anyway. I hadn't counted on having to rearrange the front display.

I pulled my phone out and dithered over whether I should call the cops first or the owner. I knew what Violet would say. "Why are you calling me? This is what I pay you for. Figure it out yourself, Miriam."

I really didn't want to have to deal with the police, but if someone had broken in and trashed the display, we'd have to file a report for insurance purposes. I stood there with my fingers hovering over the dial pad when one of the book stacks in the trashed display shifted.

A muffled chirp emanated from under the crumpled pages and bent spines. With trepidation, I started gently removing the books and various knickknacks, wincing at the ruined merchandise. I'd gotten nearly to the floor when I unearthed the source of the chirping. A feathered blue-green head with gleaming black eyes and a long, narrow beak stared up at me.

I glanced around at the mess, then back at the tiny bird. It was the largest hummingbird I'd ever seen.

"Did you do all this?"

It chirped indignantly, as if chiding me for doubting its disaster-making capabilities.

"Alright, alright, just don't bite me while I free you."

The bird chirped again, which I took as an agreement. With any luck, I could drop the little guy off at the vet down the street and still make it back in time for opening. With great care, I removed more books until I had the entire creature freed. I sat back heavily as I took in what I'd unearthed.

"You're a griffin," I squeaked.

The impossibly tiny griffin chirped and struggled to its feet. It could have fit into the palm of my hand, but I didn't think it'd appreciate being manhandled by a strange giant. The blue-green feathers on its head transitioned into a soft, creamy, fluffy fur in its cat half, and the tail deepened to blue-streaked brown at the tip. It had a deep blue patch at its throat, and its wings transitioned from green at the joint to dark blue at the tips. Unlike griffin shifters, this tiny griffin had front paws instead of bird feet. It limped towards me, favoring its right front paw. It didn't get far, as one back leg was tangled in a string of fairy lights. The wings didn't sit right, and one was definitely broken.

I couldn't believe that such a tiny thing had survived being crushed by that many books.

I rubbed my tired eyes. "I'm not getting the store open today, am I?"

The griffin chirped in response.

So much for dropping it off at the vet.

Ordinary vets weren't licensed to work on magical creatures. As soon as I brought the griffin to a vet that could help them, they'd file a report with SAID, the Supernatural Aid and Investigation Division, and then I'd have the magical police breathing down my neck, wanting to know how I came to have an injured griffin in my shop. Frankly, I wanted to know the same thing. Logic said they'd take my statement and move on, but anxiety and paranoia weren't known for listening to logic, and a little paranoid seed told me that this was going to be a far bigger deal than even my overactive imagination could come up with.

But first things first. I couldn't leave the poor guy like this.

"You're a little tangled up, aren't you?" I said sweetly. "I need you to hold real still while I get that wire unwrapped. Okay?"

The griffin chirped and settled to the ground, its tangled back leg stretched out. I'd never met a wild griffin before, but it looked like the rumors of their intelligence were true. He'd understood every word I'd said, and he was just a baby.

Continuing to talk softly, I carefully pulled at the strand of lights. It didn't take me long to free him, and when I did, he nuzzled me gently, his feathers silky soft against my skin.

"You up for a trip?" I asked as I stroked his head with my fingertip. "I've got to take you to someone who can help fix your wings and paw. I might be a fair hand at detangling strands of light, but I'm afraid my medical skills are non-existent."

He chirped again, which I took as agreement.

"You wait right there, and I'll get something to carry you in."

The griffin surged to his feet, chirping wildly, and I swear I saw panic in his eyes.

"No, no, it's okay. I'll be right back."

The wild chirping continued as he thrashed about, scrambling away.

What did I say? Something to carry him in. I suddenly felt closed-in and afraid.

"Not a cage!" I shouted desperately.

He stopped, glared at me and chirped again.

"Maybe . . ." I thought about what I had on hand. "A bowl?" I made the shape with my hands. "With something soft in it . . . like a nest."

He continued to look at me, then after a long moment, he nodded slightly. I ran back to the break room where I grabbed my plastic bowl. Normally it just held cheap lunch noodles—it was getting an upgrade today. Speaking of lunch . . . I eyed the bowl critically. It *looked* clean, but I gave it a quick wash, just to be safe.

I cast around for something soft, but the break room was sparse. I ended up sacrificing my silky infinity scarf, pouting a little as I stuffed it into the bowl. It had been a thrift store splurge last year, and if anything happened to it, I wouldn't be able to replace it. There was a reason I ate cheap ramen most days.

"Lives are worth more than things," I reminded myself as I arranged it into a nest-like formation.

The scarf was too big for the bowl, and parts of it hung out over the sides, but it'd have to do. There was no way I was going to cut it down to size.

I hurried back out to the baby griffin, who sat on the floor, his creamy, fluffy tail twitching. He'd laid his head on his good front leg, and his eyes were closed.

"Poor baby," I tutted. "You had a rough night. Alright, I'm just gonna scoop you up, real gentle now and put you in here."

It was delicate work, trying to pick up such a tiny creature while avoiding touching both wings and one leg. Eventually though, I had the griffin settled in the bowl, and he promptly curled up, resting his head on the edge. I winced internally—that was a very thin edge and couldn't possibly be comfortable, even with the scarf padding it.

"Now for the hard part," I muttered as I gingerly carried him over to the front desk. "I'm afraid I don't know any magical vets off the top of my head, so I'm going to have to look one up. That might take a few minutes. Then I'll have to secure transportation. I don't have a car, so I usually just take public transport. I'll have to figure out what buses and trains to take to get there. Unless there's one close by and I can walk."

Unfortunately, calling a cab was out of the question . . . and my budget.

"But we'll worry about that after we've found a vet for

you."

I wasn't sure why I felt the need to explain all of that to the griffin, but he chirped in agreement as if he'd understood every word.

I pulled my phone out and began searching for magical vets. Just my luck—there were none in my small city. I'd have to cross several miles of desert, either north or south, to get to the closest one, and one of the two was closed.

"South Phoenix Magical Veterinary Clinic it is," I muttered as my finger hovered over the 'call' button.

Calling people on the phone stressed me out. It was just talking to a person, and I did that every day at my job—I even answered the phone here regularly (it was, perhaps, my least favorite part of the job). I took a deep breath as I slipped into Customer Service mode. CS Miriam could handle anything, any difficult customer, phone call, situation, you name it. Of course, she'd crash and burn at the end of the day and need several hours with a good book to recover, but whatever.

I pressed the button before I could chicken out. I could do this. After all, it wasn't like I was scheduling an appointment for myself—those were ten times harder. The phone rang and rang, and just when I thought it was going to switch over to voicemail, a perky receptionist answered.

"Good morning! Thank you for calling South Phoenix Magical Veterinary Clinic," the man said. "Can I get your name?"

I couldn't help but grin at the customer service voice I heard coming over the phone. I doubted he sounded like this in real life.

"Hi, this is Miriam Jacobs from The Booklight. I found an injured baby griffin in the shop when I came in this morning, and I was wondering if I'd be able to bring him by for you to check out."

"I'm so sorry to hear about your baby griffin. And where is the mother?"

"I don't know. Like I said, he's not mine. I just found him."

"Okay. Is he bleeding?" I could hear the sound of a keyboard clacking over the phone.

"Not visibly. But one wing is definitely broken, and he favors his right front leg."

"Alright. We advise you to bring him in ASAP for one of our specialists to examine. How soon can you be here?"

I blew out a long breath. "A couple hours. I'll have to take public transit as I'm out in Wellspring without a car."

There was a long pause.

"I see. That is not ideal. Do you have anyone that can give you a ride, or will let you borrow their car?"

Gee, why didn't I think of that?

"No, sorry."

That was the problem with cutting ties and running out to live in the middle of the desert, where I didn't know anyone. My only real contact here was my boss, and she was on vacation half the time.

"Can you get a cab?"

"I have three dollars in my bank account."

Another long pause.

"We'll see you as soon as you get here, but it really is imperative that you get here as soon as possible."

I gritted my teeth. Of course I knew that! I was forgoing a day of pay just to bring the griffin in! If I'd had the money to spend on a cab, I would have—no creature deserved to be in pain longer than necessary.

I thanked him as politely as I could manage and then hung up.

"Jerk."

I took a few deep breaths as I looked up the train and bus schedules.

"Alright buddy, if we book it, we should be able to catch the next bus, which means we'll catch the next train."

Chapter 2

Miriam

I SHIFTED NERVOUSLY and checked that my precious cargo was entirely covered by my scarf. The last thing we needed right now was someone getting overly excited or concerned by the fact that I'd brought a baby griffin on the train. Also, I didn't want to risk the conductor kicking me off the train for bringing an animal, even if I was taking it to the vet. Service animals and familiars were allowed. Random wild animals, not so much.

Thankfully, the little guy seemed more interested in sleeping than causing a scene. If he just slept the whole ride into Phoenix, that'd be golden. I wondered if I should be concerned that he was sleeping, given his condition, or if it was the best thing for him.

I shook my head, trying to calm my anxious thoughts. It was rush hour, and the train was crowded—I usually preferred to ride during the off hours, partially for comfort and partially because crowds seemed to trigger my seizures. My doctors said it was because crowds triggered my anxiety, and my anxiety triggered my seizures. These seizures were the reason I didn't have a driver's license.

When the conductor came by, I quietly showed him my AZ Trax pass, which allowed me to ride all public transportation in the state. The yearly pass cost a pretty penny upfront but saved me a lot in the long run.

Before I'd left the shop, I'd texted my boss, letting her know something had come up and I wouldn't be able to open the shop today. She simply texted back, reminding me that I had no PTO and wouldn't be paid if I took today off.

I sighed and prayed for a miracle. Jobs were scarce in Wellspring—well-paying ones even more so. At least she hadn't told me I was out of a job.

Soon enough, we were pulling into our stop. When the doors opened, I was one of the first ones out, trying to beat the jostling crowd. I looked for the bus I needed, and my heart sank when I saw it pulling away.

"Two minutes," I grumbled. "You couldn't have waited two minutes for the train to get here?"

I understood they had a schedule to keep, but pulling out as the train was pulling in was just a jerk move. I hope somebody filed a complaint—not me though, never me. With an annoyed sigh, I dug my phone out of my bag and looked up the directions to the vet clinic.

Now that I wasn't taking public transportation, I could take a more direct route. Luckily, it wasn't too far away, but it was still a good fifteen-minute walk. Several other commuters, it seemed, had the same idea as me, and I joined a stream of people leaving the station.

"Nice weather for a walk," a voice said beside me.

I looked over to find a handsome, russet-haired, freckled

and tanned elf walking beside me. He had a lopsided grin, green eyes, and a largish nose. The other elves I'd seen had been almost ethereal in their beauty—he wasn't beautiful by elven standards, but he seemed more *real* somehow. He pulled a rolling briefcase behind him and carried a potted plant under one arm.

My mind conjured the bizarre image of him lounging on a couch while grading papers and wearing old fluffy bunny slippers.

"Yeah, thank goodness for that," I agreed, mentally shaking the image from my mind.

"Where are you headed?"

"The vet clinic," I responded. "I found an injured … bird this morning. You?"

He nodded genially. "That's nice of you to take the bird in—not many people would. I'm headed to the university to give a lecture on considerations of soil morphology in the creation and maintenance of magical forests."

"I guess that explains the plant." I had a feeling if I attended that lecture, I'd be completely lost.

"This is Liza. I bring her to every lecture—at least then there's one friendly face. Not that she has a face … but anyway …" he trailed off. "Sorry, these things make me nervous."

I smiled at him. "Talking on the phone makes me nervous. I can't imagine public speaking. I'd probably faint or something."

"I haven't fainted yet," he said, flashing me a grin, "but one time, I got up to speak, and the first thing out of my mouth was the loudest belch I've ever had. Right into the microphone."

"That's terrible!" I was caught between feeling mortified for him, and wanting to laugh at the absurdity of it.

He shrugged. "It was one heck of an icebreaker, though. I figured after that, anything that came out of my mouth had to be an improvement."

I grinned. "I guess that's one way to look at it."

"I'm Lucas, by the way," he said, letting go of his briefcase and extending his hand towards me.

I transferred the bowl to one hand and shook his hand as his briefcase rolled away.

"Miriam. Your lecture notes are making a break for it." I nodded at the briefcase.

He dropped my hand and dashed after the runaway briefcase, barely managing to catch it before it fell off the sidewalk.

"Nice save."

"Thanks, Miriam." He looked a bit sheepish. "The lecture doesn't start for another hour and a half, and it's free to the public. If you've got time, you're welcome to come."

"Thanks for the invitation, but I have a feeling this is going to take a lot longer than an hour and a half." I gestured with the bowl.

The griffin chirped in agreement.

Lucas nodded in understanding. "The offer still stands. Come at the beginning, middle, or even the last five minutes—you're welcome any time. Bring the bird if you want."

"Thanks." I wondered why he was so insistent on inviting me—it's not like I'd understand anything he talked about anyway.

We walked the next few minutes in silence until he had to turn into the university campus.

"It was nice meeting you, Miriam."

"You too." I waved as he walked away. "He seemed nice," I said once he was out of earshot.

The griffin chirped in agreement, then let out a plaintive cry when I tripped over a crack in the sidewalk.

"Sorry," I said with a grimace. "I'll be more careful."

***

"Hi, I'm Miriam. I called earlier about the injured baby griffin I found," I said when I got to the front desk.

"Yes, we've been expecting you," the male elf said. "Please sign in and take a seat right over there."

I dutifully signed my name and sat down in one of the chairs, cradling the bowl gently in my lap. Now that we were here, I uncovered the griffin, so I could keep a better eye on him. The little guy raised his head and let out a tiny chirp. I gently stroked his head with my fingertip.

"We made it. The lovely folks here are going to help you get all better."

I heard the rustle of wings and felt a weight settle on my shoulder. I turned my head to get a face full of brilliant orange and gold plumage. The phoenix on my shoulder bent his head to get a better look at my tiny charge.

"He's not for eating," I said, covering the bowl with my hand.

"Phil!" an exasperated voice said. "Come here. You do not need to butt your nose into everyone else's business."

The phoenix let out a melodic warble.

"Yes, it's a beautiful nose, but that doesn't mean it belongs in other people's business."

Phil warbled again. Clearly, he disagreed. His owner, a petite woodland fae with delicate antlers, hurried over. Despite being fae, something about her put me in mind of bears.

"I'm sorry about Phil. He really is just curious." She held her arm out, and Phil obligingly hopped over to it.

"No worries. He's gorgeous."

She rolled her eyes. "Don't let him hear you say that—it'll go straight to his head." She nodded at my bowl. "What ya got there?"

"Very tiny baby griffin."

She looked into the bowl and whistled. "He's a cutie. What happened to his wing?"

"Picked a fight with a stack of books and lost."

She winced. "Poor guy. He's so tiny—looks like a hummingbird. Is he a dwarf variety? Do their beaks change when they get older?"

I see where Phil gets it from.

I shrugged. "I don't know—I just found him this morning,

buried under a pile of books."

"Heck of a way to find your familiar."

I shook my head hurriedly. "No, no, he's not mine. I'm just human. I really did just find him this morning. I was hoping the vet knew of a rescue that would take him."

"Oh, sorry! I thought you were a shifter. With how calm he is, I just assumed ... sorry again." Her face was bright red.

"It's fine," I assured her. "Shifters are generally attractive, so I'll take that as a compliment. As for him, it's probably shock or exhaustion."

I wished I was a shifter, because then this cutie could have been my familiar, but humans didn't get familiars. Something about our lack of magic prevents the familiar bond from taking hold.

She nodded, still visibly embarrassed, then wandered back to her seat on the other side of the room.

"Miriam Jacobs," a vet tech called.

I quickly stood and followed her back to the exam room, where the vet was already waiting for us.

"So, you're the young lady that found an injured baby griffin," the hulking troll said, spearing me with a look.

I gulped, fighting the urge to run. I nodded. "Yes. The front display was all messed up—"

He cut me off with an upraised hand. "I'm not interested in the story. That's SAID's department. All I care about is the griffin. I take it he's in the bowl?"

I nodded again.

"Just put the bowl on the table for me, and let's see what we've got."

I complied with shaking hands.

The troll vet looked into the bowl. "My, aren't you a beauty," he said softly.

It was fascinating to watch his complete change in demeanor with the griffin. I wondered if he didn't like humans specifically or if he didn't like people in general. He gently brushed the griffin's broken wing. The griffin hissed and stabbed at him with his needle-like beak. The vet yanked his hand out of harm's way. I idly wondered how much damage the griffin's beak could really do to the troll's thick skin, but figured it was best not to ask.

"We're going to need a full-body x-ray, which means we'll have to move you. I need you to let me touch you," he said gently.

The little griffin screeched at him and struggled to his feet while attempting to stab the troll vet again.

The vet looked at me. "How did you manage to move him without becoming a bloody mess?"

I shrugged, at a loss. "I don't know. I just asked if I could move him, and he was totally chill. He never tried to stab me."

"Interesting." He stroked his chin. "Pick up the little guy and his bowl and follow me to the x-ray room. Also, you should know that he isn't a baby at all. I believe he's a variety known as a pixie griffin, or, to be politically correct, a teacup griffin. I'll need a complete examination to be sure, but the beak is telling."

I picked up the makeshift nest and followed the troll out, feeling bewildered. How could such a tiny thing be fully grown? Then again, he seemed to be half hummingbird, and those were *teeny*.

The clue was right there in front of my face the entire time.

The vet led me into a decent-sized room with a variety of machines. I had no idea what any of them did, but I was certain at least one of them was an x-ray machine. A vet tech rushed over and threw a clean sheet over a table. There was a giant 'X' in tape on the floor in front of it.

"Put him on the table there—no bowl," the vet said.

I assumed when he said 'no bowl,' he meant no scarf as well, so I carefully extricated the little guy and set him down. He let out a little *cheep* when I stepped back.

"Wait in the hallway," the troll instructed.

I turned to leave, and the griffin went berserk, cheeping and screeching wildly and struggling to flap his injured wings. I fought the desire to rush back to the table and cuddle the griffin close.

"Thought so," the troll said, looking at the griffin. He speared me with another glance, then pointed to the 'X'. "Stand there."

Confused, I did as I was told, and the griffin settled down immediately.

Turning his attention back to the griffin, the vet said, "We're going to be taking pictures of your bones. You need to hold very still so the pictures turn out good." He glanced at me expectantly.

"What?"

He rolled his eyes. "Repeat what I said to him."

"Uh, you're going to take x-rays, and he needs to hold still?"

He snorted. "New familiars. You'll get the hang of it."

"He's not my familiar," I protested. "I'm just the one that found him."

"He thinks otherwise," the troll grunted.

"But I'm human. I can't have a familiar."

The troll leaned over and practically stuck his nose in my hair. He inhaled deeply, then scrunched his nose and snorted. "Yes, definitely human. Well, stranger things have happened. You probably have supernatural blood somewhere in your line."

The griffin cheeped.

"No, it's fine. He just doesn't like people." The words bypassed my brain and spilled out of my mouth. I clamped my mouth shut in horror.

The troll vet laughed. "That's the sum of it. You pick up fast. Just talk to him about what's happening and keep him calm."

I nodded—I could do that. The tech handed me a thick apron for protection. Then, while the vet and tech worked, I rambled about anything that came to mind. And what came to mind was the plot of the last book I'd read. After several minutes of talking and far too many spoilers, I was desperately searching for another topic.

"All done," the tech said. "Go ahead and take your familiar

back to the exam room while we look over the images."

I wanted to protest again, but that seemed like a waste of breath. Humans couldn't have familiars, no matter how much they wanted one. I gently scooped the little griffin up and put him back in the bowl with the scarf, then returned to the exam room to wait.

Teacup Griffins

Location:

Also known as the Pixie Griffin, Teacup Griffins are native to Central America, ranging from southeast Mexico to northwest Colombia. Though their native habitat spans a range of over 2,200 miles, Teacup Griffins are an endangered species, with only a handful of sightings in the wild every year.

Appearance:

Averaging just shy of four inches (minus the tail), Teacup Griffins are the smallest known species of griffin. Traditionally thought to have the avian top half of a hummingbird, recent research indicates that given their decurved bill and the shape of their wings, their avian half more closely resembles that of the Cyanerpes lucidus (common name: Shining Honeycreeper).
Unlike most other species of griffins, Teacup Griffins have feline front paws as opposed to avian talons. They are also the only griffin species whose feline half closely resembles that of a domesticated cat.
Males of the species have blue avian heads, frequently with a black throat and chest patch. Their wings transition from deep blue to black at the tips. Their feline most frequently resembles a Russian Blue Felis catus, though a few gray tabbies have been reported.
Females of the species are lighter in color, with a buff base and brilliant blue malar striping, and a deep blue throat patch. Their wings gradually transition from a stunning green to deep blue. With a fluffy tail that transitions from buff to dark brown, and dark brown paws, the feline half of the females resembles a Ragdoll Felis catus.

Chapter 3

Miriam

"HERE'S THE DEAL," the troll said, sliding x-ray images onto a lighted board, "one wing is broken, and the other is fractured. Her right front forepaw is sprained. Given how you found her, we're lucky it isn't worse. However, her bones are hollow and very tiny, which makes the process of setting them *extremely* difficult. Furthermore, given her condition, our treatment options are limited. Once she's laid her eggs, we'll have other options for pain management and healing, should the first ones not work."

"Wait ... *her* ... EGGS?!" I felt like I was drowning in the information the troll was throwing at me.

"Yes, eggs. And you'll want to find her mate. It's unusual for an already-mated griffin to form a familiar attachment. As I'm sure you know, griffins mate for life—that's true of all forms of griffins, shifters and creatures, even the teacup variety. Do you have any idea where he is?"

I shook my head. "I'm not even sure how she managed to get into the bookstore."

"Either way, mated griffins do best when they are together. Long periods of separation cause stress on both parties. For now, we'll sedate her while we set her wing and splint it. We'll bind the other wing and the paw. Then we'll send you home with some healing salve and medicine, as well as information on how to care for your new familiar."

I nodded, seeing a much bigger problem looming in front of me, the tears beginning to prick my eyes.

"I can't afford any of this," I whispered. Would they take her away from me when they realized I couldn't take care of her? And what about her mate? How was I supposed to find him?

"I figured," the troll grunted. "I started an application for financial relief for familiar care. I already filled out the medical portion. You just need to fill out your personal and financial information."

He passed me a clipboard with a thick stack of paper. "You work on that while we work on her. You'll also want to think of a name for her. You can't just call her 'the griffin' on the form."

"Chrysocolla," I said immediately. "Chrys for short." At the vet's funny look, I added, "It's a blue-green gemstone. My dad is a geologist."

"Cute," the troll grunted.

Chrys chirped in approval.

"I'm glad you like it. The vet needs to make you sleep for a bit while he works on you. You'll wake up in a lot of bandages, and you won't be able to move well, but that's to keep your wings stable while they heal. After that, I guess you'll be going home with me." I looked at the vet for confirmation, and he nodded.

"I'll go get one of the techs to help me. We'll sedate her in the room and carry her back for surgery. You just focus on that mountain of paperwork. You can fill it out in the waiting room while we work."

The tech must have been waiting outside because all the vet had to do was open the door. They placed Chrys in a clear container, and within moments, she had fallen asleep. Then they carried her out, and I felt like they were taking a piece of my heart with me.

With resignation, I trudged back to the waiting room to do just that ... wait. I fiddled with the pen for a few minutes before filling out the lengthy form. There was a mind-numbing amount of information to fill in, but none of it was terribly difficult. The personal information was easy, but the financial information made me want to cry. How was I going to afford to feed Chrys when I could barely afford to feed myself? I could only hope I qualified for enough financial aid to cover more than just the vet bills.

***

One of the techs summoned me back to one of the exam rooms just after I signed the last line.

The vet had placed Chrys back in her nest bowl, my scarf pillowing her tiny body. She looked limp and lifeless.

"Before you leave, I'll need to give you at-home care

instructions for Chrys," he said, sitting on the large spinning stool. He told me about the different medications he was prescribing Chrys and the dosage. Most of what he said went over my head, but he assured me the information was all in the take-home packet.

"I want you back here in five days for a follow-up visit. Do not touch the bandages unless necessary and try to avoid getting them wet. You can give Chrys a spongebath ... er, q-tip bath, to keep her clean, but do not soak the bandages. Provided everything goes according to plan, we should be able to take her bandages off on your follow-up visit on Monday. However, strictly no flying for the next three weeks, and I want her to stay off that paw for the next two days. If you have any concerns, or she seems to get worse, don't hesitate to come back in.

"Now, while teacup griffins can have sugar water, nectar is better for them. If you are able to, plant some shrubs in your yard, or in a pot on a patio, hanging basket, whatever. The information packet will list the ones that are best for them. Do not use any insecticide or chemical spray on them. Further, teacup griffins also need to eat a variety of fresh fruits and insects. While she is recovering and nesting, you will be responsible for providing all of her dietary needs. Do not give her cut flowers from the store, as there is too great a risk of insecticide poisoning. In fact, warn her not to drink from any flower until you have made sure they are insecticide-free."

I nodded, my head reeling from the deluge of information.

"I'll take those forms from you. We'll discharge you after Chrys wakes up. Until then, please take Chrys to the recovery room. A tech will bring you your information packet and after-care instructions. Try to read through all of it before you leave."

I nodded again, feeling like I might need a minute to process everything that was just thrown at me. The vet stood, and I followed suit, walking over to scoop Chrys and her nest up. The tiny bandages drowned her and made my heart hurt.

"When do you think she'll lay her eggs?" I asked.

The vet shrugged. "It's hard to say, but soon. Your information packet should be able to tell you more. Truth is, I'd never treated or even *seen* a teacup griffin until today. They're rare, and not native to this part of the world."

My brow furrowed at that. "Then how did she get here?"

The troll nodded. "That's the question."

He showed me to the recovery room and promptly left me there. It was a medium-sized room with a handful of chairs scattered around the perimeter. A water cooler stood in one corner with a stack of paper cups on top and a small magazine rack beside it. The only other occupant was a middle-aged man with a glowing purple dog on his lap.

I picked a chair on the opposite side of the room and sat down. I'd only been sitting for a few seconds when one of the vet techs hurried in and handed me a thick stack of pamphlets and papers. If I'd known I'd be schlepping an unbound textbook home with me, I'd have brought my backpack.

With a resigned sigh, I picked up the first set of stapled pages and got started. It was the after-care guide, and it basically told me everything the vet had, but with greater detail. The next set of pages was a summary of the visit, the reason, diagnosis, and treatment. Also included were snapshots of the x-rays. Even my untrained eye could pick out the broken wing—it looked incredibly painful. I had no idea how Chrys had managed to remain calm when she was in so much pain.

I absently stroked her head with the tip of my finger as I continued to read. I didn't know how, but I was going to make sure that Chrys had the very best care. I still didn't believe she was my familiar, but somehow, I'd been tasked with taking care of this incredible creature, and I was determined to do my best.

Speaking of best, I pulled out my phone and searched for the nearest pet store. With any luck, they'd have a small, cheap package of insects I could buy for Chrys. Surprisingly, there was a small pet food store on the university campus. The next closest was a mile away, in the opposite direction of the train station.

"Looks like I'm going back to school," I joked.

Chapter 4

Miriam

I STEPPED OUT OF THE CLINIC with a bag containing medicine and a thick sheaf of papers hanging from my arm. Thankfully, they were able to defer payment until the financial aid came through. I gently cradled Chrys' bowl in my hands as I wondered how my life had gotten so crazy. Chrys chirped, and I looked down at her.

"Yeah, let's go get you some food."

On my way to Familiar Feed, I quickly checked my bank account. $3.48. I grimaced. Hopefully there was a very small and cheap package of insects for Chrys, and with any luck, it would last until my next paycheck.

I turned onto the campus and had to consult my map several times as I navigated the maze that was the university. I stepped into the feed shop and looked around for a section helpfully labeled 'insects,' but didn't immediately see anything.

"Can I help you find anything?" a clerk asked.

I jumped, and Chrys let out a reproachful chirp when I jostled her bowl.

"Sorry," I muttered to her.

"No, I'm sorry. I didn't mean to startle you," he said. "Can I help you find anything?" His nametag said 'Tony.'

"No, I—well, yes. I'm looking for small feeder insects for my ... familiar." Even though Chrys was now officially registered as my familiar, I felt like a fraud saying it out loud.

"Of course. Right this way. We don't have a huge selection, but we should have something for you."

I followed him to a shelf on the far side of the store. The crickets were obviously too large for Chrys, but the small mealworms looked just right. I picked out the container of twenty-five mealworms for $2.99 and crossed my fingers that taxes wouldn't push it over budget.

"If you upgrade to the larger container of seventy-five for $6.99, you get a better deal per worm."

"I know—I just can't afford it right now. Maybe after my next paycheck."

"Understandable. Can I help you get anything else?"

I shook my head. "No. This is it."

A flicker of disappointment flashed across his face, and I wondered if he worked on commission.

"In that case, I can help you check out at the register whenever you're ready."

I nodded and followed him to the front. He rang me up, and I winced as I thought of the last of my money vanishing.

"If you have either a student ID or a Familiar ID, you get ten percent off your total price," he said.

I gratefully fished my new badge out of my wallet and let him scan it. I had a moment of panic that he would see me listed as a human and call me a liar, but he simply handed it back without a word, and my total went down to just below the pre-tax price. Ten percent didn't save me much on an order this small, but when you're broke, every penny counts.

"Crazy what happened to the train, right?" he said as I swiped my card.

My heart skipped a beat. "What happened to the train?"

His eyebrows raised. "I'm surprised you haven't heard—it's been all over the news and social media. A gremlin got into the engine room between here and Wellspring. Completely dismantled it—*while it was still moving.* Anyway, southbound trains are canceled until they can either fix the train or get it off the tracks."

Fantastic. I'd be stuck here until the train was running again, however long that would be.

"I've been a little busy today."

Chrys chirped in agreement. The clerk looked down at her, and surprise flashed across his face as he noticed for the first time that I wasn't randomly carrying a bowl of fabric around.

"She's so tiny! What happened to her?"

"She had a run-in with a window display," I said, fighting off visions of him calling SAID because he thought I was abusing my familiar. "Just got back from the vet. She'll be fine, just needs to take it easy for a couple weeks."

"Poor thing," he said as he cast a sympathetic glance at Chrys.

"Yeah, she's been a real trooper though."

Tony nodded. "Hope she gets better soon."

I agreed, thanked him for the insects, and left. The weather was nice, so I sat on a nearby bench with Chrys on my lap while I scrolled on my phone for updates on the train situation. Just like Tony had said, there were no southbound trains right now and no indication of when service would resume.

"What do you want to do now?"

Chrys chirped, and I felt a faint niggling of hunger that wasn't mine. After wrestling with the "easy-open" top on the mealworms, I pulled out one of the dried insects and offered it to Chrys. She chirped at me sadly.

"They're too big?"

She looked at me again and chirped. I broke the tiny insect into even tinier pieces and held the crumbs out in the palm of my hand. She scooped the pieces up greedily, then chirped at me again.

"You're ... thirsty?"

Another chirp.

"Okay, but I'm not supposed to give you plain water—I need to make sugar water. Let's go find a café and see if I can beg a cup of water and some sugar."

Ideally, I'd boil the water and sugar together so the sugar would dissolve completely and there was no risk of separation, but beggars couldn't be choosers. After some searching, I found a sleek, modern-looking café just inside a larger glass-walled building.

"Could I just get a cup of hot water, please?" I asked Chloe, the barista.

"Sure," she said with a smile as she reached for a disposable cup. "Can I get you anything else?"

I shook my head. "No, I just need to make some sugar water for my familiar." I held up the bowl slightly, and Chrys chirped, fluffing out her feathers.

"OMG! She is so cute!" I could practically see the hearts coming out of the barista's eyes. She looked over her shoulder at the other barista. "Shelby! You *have* to come see this!" She turned back to me. "What happened to her?"

"Picked a fight with a window display." She was only the third person to ask, and I was already tired of explaining it.

"Poor thing."

Shelby came over, took one look at Chrys and promptly melted.

"You're making sugar water, right? Like for hummingbirds?" Chloe asked.

I nodded.

"I have a hummingbird feeder at my house. Give me a couple minutes, and I'll whip up a batch for you. You need it at room temperature, right?"

I nodded again. "Yes, but I only have, like, fifty cents."

"No worries," Chloe said with a wink. "Water and sugar are free. I'll have it ready in two shakes."

I quietly thanked her and moved to sit at a nearby table, grateful for the generosity of strangers. As I looked around, I spotted a sign promoting 'A Tale of Two Soils: a lecture on the considerations of soil morphology in the creation and maintenance of magical forests.' According to the sign, the lecture was being given just down the hall.

A quick check on my phone showed that there were no updates on the train situation.

I looked down at Chrys. "What do you say? Want to go listen to a guy talk about dirt?"

She chirped.

"Yes, we'll get your sugar water first."

We only had to wait a few minutes for Chloe to bring the sugar water to us.

"There you are, cutie. Enjoy your meal. Get better soon."

Chrys chirped as I thanked Chloe. She delivered the sugar water in an eight-ounce cup with a lid, which I took off so Chrys could have free access to the water. I quickly tested the water with my pinky, and sure enough, it was the perfect temperature.

"It's good," I said to Chrys as I held the cup so she could drink.

She dipped her beak in, and I saw just the hint of a pink tongue flicking out. When she had slaked her thirst, I replaced the lid and scooped her up. Then, I wet a napkin in a nearby drinking fountain and cleaned her beak, just as her care instructions recommended.

Chapter 5

Miriam

I OPENED THE FIRST DOOR to the auditorium I found, hoping I could just slip into a seat in the back. I froze when I realized my horrendous mistake. This was the front. Heat flooded my face, and I was paralyzed with indecision.

Lucas noticed my entrance, and with a smile, he jerked his head towards a few empty seats in the front row.

Too late to turn back now.

Shoulders hunched and face burning with embarrassment, I scuttled over to the first empty seat. I wished the ground would open and swallow me whole. This was a mistake—I should have stayed in the café and read a book on my phone or something. Of course, my phone couldn't hold a charge, so that was a risky prospect. Maybe I should have looked for the library or something. Chances of public humiliation in a library were slim. I sat down, wondering if the stare of a thousand pairs of eyes was enough to turn me to ash.

For his part, Lucas didn't miss a beat. He continued presenting as if nothing happened. I tried to focus on the lecture, but I hardly understood a word of what he said. One thing was clear though, Lucas was passionate about the topic. He talked with such energy that he seemed to fill the stage. I felt a pang in my chest as I wished I had a job I was so passionate about.

While I loved books, my job at the bookstore wasn't *fulfilling*. Of course, maybe if I made enough money to live off, I'd feel differently. I looked down at Chrys, once again wondering how I was going to make it with another mouth to feed, even if it was such a tiny one.

You could go home, a voice whispered in my mind, sounding suspiciously like my mother.

I mentally shook my head—going home was not an option. My parents loved me—that was something I'd never questioned, but their love was suffocating. If I moved back home, I'd be subject to their rules and their *concern*. They'd check on me every ten minutes just to make sure I didn't have another *episode*, and if I did, they'd haul me to the doctor's and demand a new prescription because the one I had *clearly* wasn't working. Never mind the fact that every doctor told them that no medicine would be a hundred percent effective at preventing my seizures.

Setting out on my own had been as much an act of defiance as self-preservation. My parents believed that I would never be able to live a normal life, hold down a normal job, *be* a normal person. I couldn't drive because my seizures weren't sufficiently under control. They were a lot better than they used to be, but even with medication, I would still have a few every month. My parents hadn't let me date because *what if I had a seizure on the date?*

Tired of being told what I *couldn't* do, and determined to

live my life as normally as possible, the day I turned eighteen, I got a job on the other side of the country. I'd started out here, in Phoenix. Those first few months nearly made me throw in the towel and move back home, but I refused to go back with my tail tucked between my legs.

I'd constantly felt on the verge of a seizure, and I'd had several. I'd had to scramble to find a decent doctor. New medication helped, but it was still rough.

Then one day, in a fit of desperation, I rode the train out to the middle of nowhere. As the miles between me and the metropolis grew, the weight of the impending seizures fell away, and I could breathe easily for the first time since I moved here. When I finally stepped off the train, I found myself in the little town of Wellspring, Arizona. I wasted no time finding a job there. Finding housing was more difficult, but I eventually found a little studio apartment—and for far less than what I was paying in Phoenix.

Back then, something like this would have absolutely triggered a seizure. But right now, as I stroked Chrys' sleeping head, all I felt was my regular anxiety. Even that settled as I continued to pet my new familiar. I stopped reminiscing and turned my attention back to the lecture.

I still felt a little awkward, like I should be taking notes for a pop quiz at the end. Not that notes would have done me any good, as I didn't understand most of what Lucas said. Still, listening to him was strangely relaxing, his voice putting me in mind of ancient, tranquil forests brimming with magic. His voice was different than the few other elves I'd met, deeper and more earthy, and it suited him perfectly. I idly wondered if he'd ever considered becoming an audiobook narrator—I couldn't be the only one who'd happily listen to him all day.

Before I realized it, the lecture was over, and people were leaving. I gathered my stuff and a sleeping Chrys and stood to leave.

"Miriam, wait!" Lucas called, his voice rolling over the auditorium.

I blushed deeply, wanting to sink into the floor. He hadn't taken his mic off yet, so everyone heard him call my name. Realizing his mistake, he unhooked the mic from his ear and passed it off to one of the techs. He hurried off the stage while I stood rooted to the spot, unable to move no matter how much I wanted to.

"Hey Miriam! Uh, sorry about that." He waved vaguely at the stage. "Anyways, I'm glad you came. Um, I was, uh, going to get something to eat … if you wanted to join me. Um, my treat."

I found myself agreeing before my brain finished processing what he'd said.

Did that just happen? Did he really just ask me out on a date? Is this a date? Am I reading into this? What if he's just being friendly? So what if he is? He seems nice. What's the worst that could happen? … Murder, for one thing. I mentally shook myself—going down that mental black hole would not be helpful in the slightest. I'd just make sure that wherever we went, it was a well-lit and well-trafficked area.

He beamed at me and offered his arm before realizing my hands were full.

"I can carry your bag if you'd like," he said.

"No thanks, I've got it."

"Then at least let me get the door for you," he responded with a smile.

"I'd appreciate that, thanks."

I was glad he hadn't kept insisting on carrying my stuff for me, or worse, taking it off me anyway. This wasn't about making some "feminist" statement. I didn't know him, so I wasn't comfortable with him holding my things.

"Great! Let me just get my stuff, and we'll go." He sprinted back up to the stage and hurriedly gathered his notes, shoving them haphazardly into his briefcase. He seemed a lot more nervous now than he had when speaking in front of a large audience. He scooped up Liza, his plant, and sped back over to me.

"How'd it go with the bird?" Lucas asked as we stepped outside.

"Huh? Oh! It was …" I paused as I mentally scrambled for a word that would adequately encompass the experience. "A ride."

He raised his eyebrows in a silent invitation to continue.

"So," I said, feeling a stab of guilt, "she's actually a griffin. I just didn't want to get into the whole 'Oh my gosh! It's a griffin!' thing earlier."

"Understandable," Lucas said, his eyes flicking to Chrys' bowl with evident curiosity, but he refrained from asking, letting me continue at my own pace.

The whole story poured out of me, from when I walked into the bookshop this morning to the auditorium. I found myself telling him everything, from how excited I was to have a familiar, to how nervous I was that I wouldn't be able to care for her properly, and how a large part of me thought it was just some big mistake.

"Sorry, I didn't mean to dump all of that on you."

"Don't worry about it—that sounds like a lot to process. For what it's worth, I don't think Chrys made a mistake."

My heart ached with a desperate longing to believe him.

Chapter 6

Miriam

I SAT BACK IN THE BOOTH, humming happily and pleasantly full. I still had half a sandwich, and a slice of cheesecake left. I was amazed that Lucas had ordered not one but *two* desserts just for me. I'd been eying them for sure, but I didn't want to press my luck or make Lucas think I was taking advantage of him. And yet, he'd noticed and ordered them anyway.

"Are you sure you've had enough?" Lucas asked.

I chuckled—I hadn't eaten this much in one sitting in ages. "I ate so much you're going to have to roll me out of here."

Lucas grinned as if my answer made him happy. "Glad to hear. I'll go get boxes for the rest of the food."

By that, he meant my food, as he had managed to polish off everything on his plate. We'd ended up at a gnomish soup and sandwich shop, which was perfectly fine by me as gnomes were known for their delicious food and generous portion sizes.

Food, family, friends—gnomes have it right. Especially the food.

While Lucas was getting the boxes, I checked my phone for updates on the train situation. While it wasn't fixed yet, they at least had an ETA on when service between Phoenix and Wellspring would resume. Three hours. I just needed to figure out what to do with myself for the next three hours. I wondered if the university library had any fun books.

"What's wrong?" Lucas asked as he slid back into the booth, wax-lined cardboard boxes in hand.

I shook my head. "Nothing much. The train between here and Wellspring is out of service."

"You live in Wellspring?"

I nodded. "Yeah, I only came up here because of Chrys."

He grinned. "Small world."

"You live in Wellspring too?"

Somehow, in all of our small talk, where we lived hadn't come up. I'd just assumed that when he said he taught botany and soil science classes for the university, that meant he lived up here too.

He nodded. "Yeah. I work down there, so it just made sense to live down there too. A few times a year, I'll give a lecture up on the main campus, but for the most part, I stay down there."

"Oh!" I exclaimed when the pieces clicked together. "You teach at the Wellspring campus—the one that's located inside the conservatory?"

He nodded. "It made the most sense to put the magical botany classes there."

"I'm sooo jealous. I love the conservatory! I follow all of its social media pages, and I've probably spent hours scrolling through all of the pictures over and over again."

I clamped my mouth shut, not sure why I'd told him all of that.

I'd never been inside the conservatory (the tickets were a little outside my ramen-noodles-every-day budget), but I had walked the public grounds outside. Something about the conservatory drew me like a moth to a flame. I desperately wanted to go inside and get a ticket, just once, but I knew that if I did, I'd need to go again. I'd promised myself that once my financial situation improved, I'd get an annual pass and go so frequently that I'd know every worker by name. I couldn't even say what it was about the conservatory that drew me. I'd been to magical conservatories before with my parents, but none of them were as compelling as the Wellspring one was, and I hadn't even been inside yet—the closest I'd gotten was to the front desk to ask for a job. I felt a stab of jealousy that Lucas got to work there every day.

The conservatory was massive and Wellspring's one claim to fame. Built around several of the springs that gave our town its name, it had originally started as an eccentric elf's pet project. He'd spent years and hundreds of thousands of dollars to gather rare magical specimens and plant them with the utmost care in the micro-climates created by the magical springs. He'd willed it to the university on his death.

Lucas pouted slightly. "Unfortunately, they make me come up to campus every few semesters when I teach my beginning soil science classes."

"I'm sorry," I said, fighting back a smile, "that must be terribly upsetting."

Lucas crumpled up a clean napkin and threw it at me. I

batted it away with a laugh. Chrys chirped and I suddenly felt thirsty. Recognizing it wasn't *my* thirst, I took the lid off the sugar water and tipped it so she could have a drink.

"You'd never know you only bonded this morning," Lucas remarked with a smile.

"What do you mean?"

Lucas shrugged. "A couple of my siblings have familiars—it took them both at least a month to understand when a single sound meant 'feed me.' One even took to munching on my brother's fingers just to get the point across."

I snickered, my heart lightening. *At least I'm doing something right.*

"As for the train situation, I might have a colleague headed down to Wellspring soon. Give me a few minutes, and I might be able to get us a ride."

I wanted to protest and tell him not to go to any trouble on my account, but he was already on the phone, making a call. I shuddered inwardly—I would never understand people who *called* others voluntarily. Texting, email, even snail mail was preferable to a phone call.

"All set," Lucas said after he hung up. "We caught her just in time."

"Are you sure she doesn't mind?" I asked. "I don't want to impose."

He shook his head. "Trust me, if it was an imposition, she would have said so."

"Alright," I said, still uncomfortable. Lucas seemed nice, but was it really wise to get in a stranger's car?

Chrys popped her head over the side of the bowl and rubbed her beak along my thumb with a chirp. They say animals are good judges of character—if Chrys trusted Lucas, then it was probably fine.

With that, we gathered our stuff and headed out. We'd only been standing on the curb for a minute when a bright purple SUV pulled up in front of us.

"That's her," Lucas said as the passenger window rolled down.

Strangely, the eye-searing color of the vehicle made me more comfortable—who stages an abduction in such a noticeable vehicle?

"You'll have to get in the back—the front seat's full," a voice shouted from inside. "So's the trunk!"

As if he'd expected this, Lucas was already opening the back door. In went his briefcase and Liza—I couldn't help but smile when he buckled the plant into place. Then I passed him everything except Chrys and my purse.

"Middle or window?" Lucas asked.

"Window, please."

Lucas nodded and hopped inside, buckling himself into the middle seat. After a moment of hesitation, I passed Chrys to him so I could get in and buckle myself. As soon as I was buckled, I turned to take Chrys back and found her preening for Lucas.

"She's gorgeous," he said as he passed her back.

"I think so too."

"Why, thank you Lucas! I didn't know you felt that way

about me! But I have to let you know, I do have a girlfriend," our mysterious driver said from the front.

I looked over to find a female goblin grinning at us, her large green ears sparkling with several pairs of earrings.

Lucas simply rolled his eyes in response. "Hattie, this is Miriam. Miriam, this is Hattie—she handles all the IT stuff at the Wellspring campus. I'm pretty sure the entire campus would crash and burn without her."

"Aww, you say the sweetest things." She paused. "So, Miriam, you one of the professor's students? I don't think I've seen you around campus before."

"What? No, uh, we just met today. I went to his lecture then we got lunch after."

"Oh, so it was love at first sight? Saw him up there and thought 'yeah, I gotta get a piece of that?'" Hattie nodded in approval. "You go girl. Don't let this one get away—he's a keeper."

My face flushed with embarrassment. "That's not what I ... I mean, this isn't ... he is ... um ..." I glanced out the window in desperation. "Oh look, a tree!"

I wanted to sink into the seat in embarrassment. *A tree? How is that remotely interesting? Way to go, Miriam. You made this ten times more awkward. Gold star.*

Lucas leaned over to look out my window. "That's an alligator juniper."

My whirling thoughts ground to a screeching halt. "Alligator?"

Lucas nodded, his eyes lighting up. "They got their name

because of their distinctive bark pattern, which looks like alligator skin. They're an important part of the local ecosystem and provide food and shelter for a wide variety of wildlife, particularly birds. A type of evergreen tree, their berry-like cones are an excellent food source for many animals, particularly in the winter months when other food sources are scarce. Juniper berries have also been used in many traditional medicines and teas, and even to flavor meats."

"Thank you, professor," Hattie said dryly.

I shot Lucas a grin. "I guess Arizona has alligators after all."

He chuckled, the corners of his eyes crinkling. "Sorry, I have a tendency to info-dump when it comes to plants."

I nudged him with my elbow. "Don't apologize—I like learning new things. Also, I think Hattie would do the same if we asked her about her computers."

I was grateful for that info-dump as it successfully diffused the awkward situation I'd made, but mostly, I enjoyed listening to him talk. *Maybe he has a recorded lecture I could listen to, on repeat, any time I need to relax.*

"Truth," Hattie agreed from the front.

"Do they really make juniper berry tea?" I asked—I was a sucker for a good herbal tea. Junipers were everywhere here, and if I could gather the stuff I needed in the wild, it would make my bank account happy.

"Yes, though it is a diuretic, so be careful not to drink too much."

"Excellent first date topic, Prof. A-plus," Hattie snickered.

I grinned. "I don't mind. I was thinking of trying to make

some, just to see what it tasted like, so that was very useful information."

"See?" Lucas said, gesturing to me. "At least somebody here appreciates me. Though, if you're going to forage for berries, you'll need to be extra careful because some varieties are poisonous."

I deflated a little—I loved herbal tea, but not enough to risk accidental poisoning.

"I've got a few blends you might like, if you'd like to join me for tea sometime," Lucas said, his expression hopeful.

Is he asking me out on a second date?

I smiled, blushing. "I'd like that."

"Bold, Prof, bold," Hattie piped in. "Most people wait until the *end* of the date before risking getting shot down—you still have at least thirty minutes before we hit Wellspring."

"Thank you, Hattie," Lucas said, his tone conveying the opposite.

"Here to help," the goblin replied with a cackle.

Chapter 7

Miriam

*E*VEN THOUGH IT WAS PAST today's early closing time, I'd asked Hattie to drop me off at the bookstore. I still needed to clean up Chrys' mess, so I didn't have to come in extra early tomorrow. I stared at the mini-disaster, the piles of books, bookstands, various decorations and detritus, and took a deep breath. I had no idea how such a tiny creature had managed to create such a large mess, but I had a feeling it was only a matter of time before Chrys gave me a live demonstration.

I gently placed her bowl on the checkout counter, and Chrys gave me a sleepy *cheep!* before tucking her head and going back to sleep. Then, I rolled up my metaphorical sleeves and got to work.

I sorted the merchandise into three piles: perfectly fine, minor cosmetic defects, and total loss. The first pile was pitifully small, but thankfully, so was the third. Then I made a fourth pile for the decorations—any that were too broken to repair went straight into the garbage.

After sweeping up the debris, I sent Violet a report, along

with pictures. I packed the slightly damaged items and the completely broken ones in separate boxes and put them in the office for Violet to sort through when she had a chance. Violet gave me a lot of responsibilities in the shop, but pricing merchandise was not one of them—she probably thought I'd price everything so low she wouldn't make a profit.

Once that was done, I reshelved the few books that made it through unscathed and then spent the next several minutes untangling the fairy lights and repairing the decorations. Thankfully there weren't many that needed repairs, and the ones that needed to be tossed were primarily paper cutouts.

Now I just needed to come up with another display. I toyed with the idea of simply redoing the original, but it had already been up for a few weeks, so Violet was going to make me change it again soon anyway. I glanced over at the cause of my extra work and grinned.

It was brilliant. *Two birds, one stone.* I grimaced—I probably shouldn't use that particular idiom anymore.

Twenty minutes later, I stood in front of the bay window, a pile of books and decorations around me. I carefully taped the fairy lights around the edges of the window, working from the bottom up, making sure it was all flush with the surface. Unlike the last display, there would be no dangling strands for Chrys to get tangled in.

As I worked my way across the top of the window, something caught the corner of my eye. I taped the section I was holding and turned to look.

"So that's how you got in," I muttered when I saw the dangling vent cover.

I quickly finished the lights and moved my stool over to the vent. Unfortunately, even with the stool, I was too short to reach it.

No biggie. I needed to get the screwdrivers from the supply closet anyway. I'll just grab the ladder while I'm at it.

Just as I finished tightening the last screw, Chrys began shrieking. I looked at her in alarm, wondering how such a tiny body could make such a loud noise. The world tilted, fracturing into a dozen pieces as it slid away.

Broken images flew at me so fast I couldn't make sense of them. Encroaching shadows. Trees. Terror. Breathlessness. Birds of prey.

***

Lucas

Hattie pulled into the auto repair shop's parking lot, and I climbed out of the SUV, a stack of papers crinkling underfoot. I picked it up, grimacing at the footprint on the white paper.

"Sorry, Hattie, I stepped on your…" I trailed off as I read the title. *Teacup Griffin: Basic Care Guide.* "Never mind, this is Miriam's." I'd swing by the bookstore to give it to her before heading home.

"Did she leave it, or did you steal it so you could have an excuse to see her again?" Hattie asked with a smirk.

I rolled my eyes. "You know, not everyone is as devious as you."

She pretended to wipe a tear. "I know. It's so tragic."

I laughed. "That's one way to look at it."

"So, when are you going to bite the bullet and buy a new car?" It was a question nearly as old as our friendship.

"When this one bites the dust." My reply was as rote as her question.

"Well, you're going to need a bigger car soon," she said with a devious grin.

I was afraid to ask, but like a fool, I did anyway.

"And why is that?"

"That little thing's not big enough for all the babies you and *Miriam* will have."

I regretted asking.

"You know, humans only have *one* baby at a time." Unlike goblins, who only ever underwent one pregnancy but could have up to ten babies at once. "And my car is perfectly capable of handling one car seat."

"So you *have* been thinking about babies! Also, that's horribly inefficient."

"Bye, Hattie. Thank you so much for the ride," I said, closing the door firmly, Liza tucked under my arm.

She cackled and waved, belting, "Lucas and Miriam sitting in a tree, K-I-S-S-I-N-G," as she pulled out.

That conjured up many pleasant images, daydreams I could get lost in if I let myself. I shook the picture out of my mind— I couldn't let myself get too far ahead. She'd probably just agreed to the tea to be polite, and she'd bolt when she realized how boring I was. And unattractive. I rubbed my nose self-consciously as the taunts and jeers from my childhood rang in my ears. I didn't have the same ethereal beauty that full-blooded elves had, and I'd suffered plenty of bullying at the hands of my full-blooded peers.

More than one girl had ghosted me when they realized I wasn't cosmetically disfiguring myself to "blend in" with the humans. Others dumped me, claiming I was "too boring," as if my PhDs in soil science and botany had conjured images of a rugged adventurer exploring untamed lands, and my fluffy bunny slippers, textbooks, and houseplants were a far cry from what they'd expected. The slippers were a gag gift from Jonas, my youngest brother. Joke's on him—those slippers were *comfy*.

I wrenched myself back to the present—reminiscing about my failed dating life wasn't going to get my car paid for.

"What's the damage?" I asked the goblin mechanic as I placed Liza on the counter.

"Not too bad this time," Briggs replied. "But—"

"I know, I know," I cut him off. "It's time to start thinking of replacing it."

It's not that I couldn't afford to replace it, but this car had gotten me from high school all the way through grad school—it felt disloyal to get rid of it now.

"I wouldn't say it if it wasn't true," Briggs said. "I mean, you are my best customer."

I rolled my eyes. "You only say that because I'm in here every month."

"That's my point!" he exclaimed, waving his arms emphatically. "Your monthly repair bills are as much as a new car payment, sometimes more! Don't get me wrong, I love taking your money, but I respect you and my profession too much not to tell you how it is. Right now, you're just delaying the inevitable and increasing the chance that something catastrophic will happen when you're on the road."

I hadn't thought of it like that. "I'll start looking at other cars."

"Good, now give me your money and go kiss your girl."

My ears burned. "You heard that?"

He cackled. "My friend, the whole block heard."

"Heard what?" Trevor, Briggs' troll assistant, asked, wiping his hands on a cloth as he came in from the garage. "Hey Professor, who's Miriam?"

"Just a girl I met," I muttered, thrusting my card towards Briggs.

"She cute?" Trevor asked.

"None of your business," I snapped, Miriam's warm brown eyes flashing through my mind.

"Very cute, then," he surmised.

"You should bring her by. We need to make sure she's good enough for our favorite customer," Briggs said with a wink.

"Only if I feel like scaring her off," I grumbled, my face heating. Wasn't I too old for this kind of razzing?

"If you don't want to scare her off, I suggest getting rid of that death-trap-on-wheels," Briggs replied as he returned my card. "I'm serious—it's only barely scraping by on the safety check."

I rolled my eyes but said nothing as I took my card back and signed the receipts. Briggs passed me my keys, and Liza and I left. I buckled the fern into the front seat and pulled out of the parking lot.

I glanced over at Miriam's papers and nodded to myself. I needed to pick up dinner or something first. It was against gnomish culture to show up to a date without food. *Not that this is a date ... not that I'd mind if it was a date. It could be a date. Will be? Maybe? What kind of things would she like to do on a date?*

She'd seemed interested in the juniper berry tea and our subsequent tea date, so maybe she'd like to go foraging for tea ingredients. Or maybe she was just being polite—most women I'd met didn't consider foraging romantic, or even enjoyable. I shook my head—I was getting ahead of myself. I should just grab something from a coffee shop and head over to her work. If I spent too long dithering indecisively, she'd already be gone, and I'd have missed my chance. Besides, she needed her papers.

I bypassed the big chain coffee shops and headed to my favorite gnome-run café. The line was long, as usual, but worth the wait. I ordered my usual and an assortment of pastries, but hesitated when it came time to order a drink for Miriam—I didn't know her well enough to know her preferences. In the end, I just asked the barista to make their most popular tea. I ended up with a matcha boba tea with a towering dome of whipped cream on top. I made a mental note to come back and try it myself if Miriam liked it.

I hurried out of the café, dismayed at how long it had taken.

Hopefully Miriam was still at work. If not, maybe she'd let me swing by her place. I shook my head—that might come across as a bit stalkerish. If she wasn't in the bookshop tonight, I'd just swing by tomorrow before work.

I put the drinks in the cup holder and the pastries by Liza. "Don't eat them," I said, only half-joking. Sometimes I could swear the plant was sentient.

I drove over to the bookshop, grateful to see the lights were still on. Though the sign was flipped to 'closed,' Miriam was standing on a ladder by the window. I parked, grabbed the drinks and pastries, and stepped out of the car. Just as I reached the door, Chrys began shrieking. I jumped, startled, wondering what I'd done to set her off.

Miriam wobbled, reaching out to the ladder for support but missed. She tilted, toppling off the edge. My heart lodged in my throat as I dropped the food and wrenched the door open, everything moving like molasses.

My arms closed around her before she hit the floor, her weight sending both of us to the ground. She thrashed in my arms, moaning and whimpering. Her eyes were open, practically glowing from the bright sheen covering them. Even though she was looking right at me, I knew without a shadow of a doubt that she could neither see nor hear me.

"Run! Danger! The trees! No time! No time!"

She continued to writhe, and I carefully dragged her away from the ladder and anything else she might inadvertently hurt herself on. Not knowing what else to do and feeling completely useless, I simply held on, praying the storm would soon pass. Across the room, Chrys' shrieking subsided to concerned trills.

Chapter 8

Miriam

REALITY CRAWLED BACK, in no hurry to grace me with its presence. Along with it came the feeling of having been hit by a truck. Everything ached, and my limbs felt like lead. I blinked a few times, trying to focus on what was in front of me, but my mind stubbornly refused to make sense of it. The seizure was over, the hallucinations should be gone, and yet …

I raised my arm, the effort almost too much, and poked the specter above me. My questing finger met warm flesh.

"You're real," I whispered. *How?*

His larger, calloused hand covered mine, pressing it against his cheek. "I'm here," he said, his voice cracking. "By the stars, I thought … I thought … what happened?"

"Just a seizure," I replied, trying to shrug it off with a laugh as I waited for the inevitable pitying look. "I get them regularly."

And there it is.

"I'm sorry. That must be rough. How can I … what should

I …" he took a deep breath. "What can I do for you during your seizures?"

I smiled at him, my heart warming. Most people would start to lecture me about my seizures or give me useless advice, like "Don't have them in busy places" or "Have you tried this new miracle oil?" Rare were the people who asked what *I* wanted or needed from them.

"Stay with me, keep me safe, don't restrain me or put anything in my mouth. If you can, turn me on my side and put a pillow under my head—it'll keep me from cracking my noggin open. And finally, time the seizure—if it lasts more than five minutes, call an ambulance."

Lucas nodded. "Stay, keep safe, pillow yes, restraints no. More than five minutes, call 911. And after?"

"Mostly, just let me rest—these things take a lot out of me."

Lucas rose, taking me with him. "In that case, I'm taking you home."

I would have protested, but spending thirty minutes riding public transit only to have to drag my sorry carcass two blocks to my apartment was more than I even wanted to think about.

"I'd appreciate it, thanks."

Lucas carried me out of the store, ignoring my weak protests. He somehow gracefully opened the door and deposited me in the back seat, all without jostling me. It was truly a miraculous feat, one which I did not have the energy to fully appreciate.

"Pass me your keys—I'll lock up."

"They're on the counter, next to Chrys."

I struggled to keep my eyes open, to make sure things got locked up properly. I'd need to come in early tomorrow to clean up and get the store ready for opening. I managed to keep my eyes open long enough to see him lock the door and ensure he had Chrys with him.

"What's your address?" he asked as he set Chrys' bowl on my lap.

I tiredly rattled off the address, glad when he didn't ask me to repeat it—talking took too much energy.

I intended to just rest my eyes for a moment, but the next thing I knew, Lucas was tucking me into bed in my studio apartment. I'd be embarrassed about this in the morning, but for now, I was just grateful for the pillow under my head.

***

Lucas

I tossed the remains of the drinks and ruined pastries into the garbage with regret—I'd been looking forward to sharing them with Miriam. Then I climbed into the car and plugged her address into the GPS on my phone.

Miriam lived on the third floor in one of the few apartment buildings in Wellspring. I couldn't see an elevator, so I carried her up the three flights of stairs. Even though she was lighter than I'd expected, by the end of the first flight, I was cursing myself for not taking up weight training years ago. Eventually, I made it to her apartment without dropping her.

The back of my neck prickled as I unlocked her door. I

looked over my shoulder to see Miriam's neighbor across the way staring me down. Built like a fridge, his tattooed shoulders filled the door frame. His bulk alone made me wonder if he had any ogre blood in him, but his death stare told me that asking would be suicide.

"Afternoon," I said with a nod. He simply continued to glare at me.

I turned back to the door, my shoulders tense as I berated myself for not taking up weight training *and* martial arts years ago. I unlocked the door and slipped inside, closing it behind me with my foot.

Miriam's apartment was a cramped studio that was practically bare. The only furniture was a mattress on the floor, a folding card table piled high with library rejects, and an armchair that had seen better days. The kitchen was even more depressing. With so little counter space, I wondered how she even cooked.

I gently tucked her into bed and set her shoes by the door before returning to my car. Her neighbor was still standing in his doorway, his eyes laser-focused on Miriam's door. Even though I was only going to be gone for a few minutes, I nervously locked it behind me.

Chrys was unhappy to have been left behind and let me know of her displeasure with a sharp peck to my fingers when I picked her bowl up.

"I'm sorry. I didn't want to risk dropping you while I was carrying Miriam."

She chittered, as if scolding me.

"I know you don't like being separated from her, but it was

necessary."

I carried Chrys and the rest of Miriam's stuff up to her apartment. Her scary neighbor had disappeared, and I wasn't sure if I should be relieved or not. I set Chrys down beside Miriam, which turned out to be the right move because Chrys promptly climbed out of the bowl and curled up next to Miriam's ear, emitting a soft purr as she closed her eyes.

After a moment of hesitation, I pulled out Miriam's phone and double-tapped the power button to pull up the camera. I snapped a couple photos of her and Chrys, hoping this didn't come across as stalkerish as it felt. *The pictures are on her phone, not mine. That should help ... right?* When my older sister got her familiar, she couldn't *stop* taking pictures for a month, wanting to document *everything*. Even my younger brother, who was allergic to sentimentality, took dozens of pictures that first week. Hopefully she'd appreciate the thought behind it. Spying her charger lying on the floor, I plugged her phone in.

Then I went to the kitchen to get her a cup of water, figuring she'd be thirsty when she woke up. The first cupboard I opened was bare. I frowned. She only had three cupboards—they should all be full to bursting. I opened the second one and found four packs of cheap ramen, salt, and pepper. My frown deepened, and I opened the final cupboard. A familiar matching set of three plastic bowls, four plates, and four cups greeted me. I glanced over at Chrys' nest, the fourth bowl.

I raked a hand through my hair as I grabbed a cup and quietly shut the cupboard door. The fridge was an older model with no water dispenser, so I checked inside for filtered water. The bare shelves mocked me. The only things in her fridge were a handful of condiments.

I turned the sink faucet on and cupped my hand under the stream. I took a tentative sip, then filled the cup.

At least her water's fine.

When I turned to put the cup beside her bed, I realized my mistake. With a defeated sigh, I put the cup back on the counter—I couldn't risk it on the floor next to her phone.

I spied a closet door beside the kitchen I hadn't noticed before. Feeling like a snoop, I opened it, hoping this was where she stashed all her stuff. My hope was in vain. I found a few empty shelves, a towel, a bottle of laundry detergent, and an all-in-one washer and dryer unit—Mom hated those. I closed the door with a soft *click*.

With a final glance at Miriam, I grabbed her keys and slipped out the door, locking it behind me.

Chapter 9

Lucas

"LUCAS! WE WERE JUST TALKING ABOUT YOU! How'd your presentation go today? Have you been getting enough to eat?"

I held the phone away from my ear—Mom seemed to think her voice wouldn't carry over the phone unless she was yelling.

"I'm fine, Mom. The presentation went great. Yes, I've been getting enough to eat. I need your advice on something, though. There's this girl—"

I nearly dropped my phone at the sound that came out of it.

"A GIRL?! Oh, Lucas, I'm so happy for you! What's her name? When are you bringing her home? What's her favorite food? Does she have any allergies?"

"Slow down, Mom. It's not like that. It is about food, though."

"You need my baklava recipe as an offering before you ask her out?"

"No, that's not what … actually, if you're offering, I would love that recipe." Only a fool turned down Mom's baklava recipe. "That's not why I called, though. She had a seizure, and when I helped her back to her apartment, I discovered that she doesn't have any food. Unless, of course, you consider four packages of cheap ramen to be food. But it's not just that. There were no spices or seasonings, not even sugar and cinnamon, only salt and pepper. The fridge was empty of everything except condiments, and those were mostly empty." I took a deep breath. "What do I do? I want to help her, but…"

"But you don't want her to feel like a charity case," Mom finished for me.

"Yeah."

"Alright, here's what you're going to do," she said, then outlined her plan.

"That is a scarily detailed plan for having five seconds to think about it," I said when she finished. "You've done this before, haven't you?"

"I've done it, your grandmother has done it, a few of your aunts and uncles, and several other gnomes as well. Feeding people's in our blood. I'm proud of you, Son."

My heart warmed. "Thanks, Mom."

"And who knows, maybe this time next year, I'll have a new daughter to welcome to the family. And maybe even a grandbaby on the way."

"Bye, Mom." I hung up, the tips of my ears burning. *And it had been going so well.*

I climbed out of the car and grabbed a few reusable shopping bags from the trunk. I jotted down a list as I headed into the grocery store.

***

Miriam

This was one of the most vivid dreams I'd ever had. I could *smell* the bacon sizzling—that's how I knew it was a dream. That, and a handsome man cooking in my kitchen, was so far out of the realm of reality that it was laughable. His russet hair brushing the tips of his pointed ears. He moved confidently and with purpose, humming to himself as he cooked. The only thing that would make this better was if he was shirtless. I smiled at the thought, and the dream slipped away.

Chapter 10

Miriam

A LOUD, INCESSANT BEEPING yanked me from pleasant dreams about shirtless elves and bacon. I rolled out of bed and stumbled to the kitchen, blinking blearily as I tried to locate the source of the noise. Somewhere behind me, Chrys chirped in annoyance. I completely empathized.

The sound turned out to be the oven timer. I pressed the button to turn it off, then stared at it in confusion. *Why was it beeping? Did some sort of sensor get tripped?* That's when I noticed the slow cooker on the counter to the left of my stove. I stared at it in deepening confusion—I didn't own a slow cooker. I spied a piece of paper beside the new appliance and picked it up, hoping it would shed some light on the situation.

> Miriam,
>
> The timer is for the slow cooker. When it goes off, enjoy some of my mom's famous breakfast casserole, or put it in the fridge to enjoy later. There's

more cheese in the fridge, as well as other toppings. Hope you're feeling better.

Text me,

Lucas

I lifted the lid and inhaled the heavenly scent. I almost cried at the sight. This was enough food to feed me for days. Even though I was exhausted and wanted to crawl back into bed, I wasted no time scooping some onto a plate. Then I opened the fridge, wondering about the toppings Lucas mentioned. There, staring back at me, were containers of guacamole, sour cream, and shredded cheese, as well as half a package of uncooked bacon, and a carton of eggs.

I spooned some guacamole and sour cream onto my egg casserole and sobbed as I ate. I couldn't remember the last time someone cooked for me. This was more than just buying me a muffin for breakfast, which would have been thoughtful enough. But this, this was so much more.

Gnomes believed you could *taste* the love in homemade food, and in that moment, I believed it. The food warmed me up from the inside out, soothing away the aches the seizure left me with in a way that no medicine could. I licked my plate clean and barely stopped myself from getting a second helping. I didn't know when I'd have food like this again—I needed to stretch it as far as I could.

I dropped my plate in the sink, promising myself I'd wash it later and put the rest of the casserole in the fridge. Then I shuffled back to bed. My alarm for work hadn't gone off yet, and I needed as much rest as I could get. After pulling the quilt up to my ears, I reached down, grabbed my phone and fired off a quick text to Lucas, thanking him for the food. Hopefully it wasn't too early for him.

"Night, Chrys," I murmured, already halfway asleep.

***

Bzzzz. Bzzzzz. Bzzzz.

The vibrating phone pulled me out of a dreamless sleep, and I silenced it with a groan. I cracked my eyes open and glared at the offending device. I sat up and stretched, feeling better than I'd expected, but still not great. The day after a seizure usually left me feeling like I'd been hit by a truck. Today was downgraded to "tumbled down a flight of stairs." Good food usually helped the symptoms abate faster, but there was practically nothing to eat here.

Wait…

I whipped my head around to look at the fridge so fast I might have given myself whiplash.

I do have good food … unless that was a dream.

The slow cooker base still sat on the counter, confirming it wasn't a dream. I scrambled out of bed and tripped over my feet in my haste to get to the fridge, barely managing to catch myself and avoid face-planting on the worn carpet.

Chrys scolded me loudly from the bed.

"I know. I know. I'll be more careful."

Despite my promise to Chrys, I still rushed to the fridge and yanked the door open. There, on the top shelf, sat a black ceramic slow cooker with a little bit of heaven inside. I grabbed a clean plate and dished myself a hearty scoop. While it heated in the microwave, I re-read Lucas' note, noticing a post-script I hadn't seen last night.

>P.S. Chrys' food is in the pantry.

My insides were as gooey as the cheese on my breakfast. He wasn't just taking care of me, but my familiar as well. I shuffled over to the pantry, most of my energy being sapped by my mad dash to the fridge. I opened the door and promptly burst into tears. He hadn't just made a cup of sugar water for Chrys—he'd bought a hummingbird feeder with little perches. When she was healed, I could hang it from the ceiling. Beside the feeder sat a jar of sugar water and a bag of pure organic cane sugar.

I pulled out my phone to thank Lucas for the food and saw the last message I'd sent him.

> **Me:** You are an angel, and the food is heavenly. Marry me.
>
> **Lucas:** Glad you liked it. ☺

My face burned as I quickly slid the phone back into my pocket. I couldn't believe I'd proposed to him over text after knowing him for less than a day. Though, to be fair, the breakfast casserole was *that* amazing.

Thankfully, the beeping microwave saved me from a spiral of embarrassing thoughts. When I grabbed the guac and sour cream, I noticed another thing I hadn't last night—a punnet of raspberries. I quickly rinsed them and put a few on a plate for Chrys.

I tried hard to savor the food, but before I knew it, my plate was empty and my belly pleasantly full.

Chrys' pain-filled scolding reached me, and I grimaced. I'd been selfish—I should have seen to her needs first.

"I'm sorry, love. Let's get you taken care of."

I walked over to the bed and moved Chrys to the counter. After measuring out the first medicine and mixing it with a little sugar water, I offered it to Chrys, who drank it, though an itch at the back of my mind told me she thought it tasted funny.

"I know, sweet girl. Medicine usually tastes pretty gross. Lucas left you a feeder full of untainted sugar water you can drink from whenever you want. Are you ready for your pain medicine?"

She chirped in the affirmative and obediently opened her beak when asked. I carefully used the dropper to put two drops in her mouth, though my hand shook so much I was surprised they both went in.

Chrys gagged and rubbed her beak against her bandages, letting me know how awful the medicine tasted.

"Sorry. I've got some insects and fruit if you want to wash the taste out of your mouth."

She chirped in the affirmative, and I crumbled up a

mealworm next to her raspberries. I lifted her out of her nest and set her directly on the plate with the food. Then, I grabbed the hummingbird feeder and placed it on the counter next to her, so she could reach all of her food without having to get up.

A glance at the clock showed I was running later than I'd expected, and I needed to get in early to finish the window display. I left Chrys enjoying her food and hopped in the shower. The hot water felt heavenly and soothed some of the residual aches my seizure left me with. I closed my eyes for just a moment to enjoy the nearly-scalding water pummeling my sore muscles.

BEEP! BEEP! BEEP!

I jolted back to reality. Quietly cursing myself for drifting off, I sped through the rest of my morning routine. I threw my hair into a bun and brushed my teeth while cleaning Chrys' beak and the whole counter from the mess she'd made while eating the raspberries. The jar of sugar water, Chrys' medicine, bugs, and berries all went into a backpack I dug out from under a stack of books. I dumped the rest of the contents of my purse into one of the pockets and slung the bag onto my back.

I scooped Chrys and her nest up and rushed out the door, praying with everything in me that I wouldn't be late.

Chapter 11

Miriam

I SANK ONTO THE BUS SEAT, struggling to regulate my breathing. I'd run from my apartment to the bus stop and barely made it in time. Chrys chirped at me reproachfully from her nest. Thankfully, it was quiet enough that the other commuters didn't notice, or if they did, they didn't care enough to say anything. My breathing finally returned to normal as we pulled up to my stop.

I walked down the street to The Booklight and fumbled in my pocket for the keys. Violet was on vacation for a few more days, which meant I was stuck opening *and* closing until she got back. I was glad Chrys' mishap yesterday didn't cause any major damage because I didn't want to have to handle that. I was also grateful for the bigger paycheck the overtime would mean.

I slipped through the door and deposited Chrys on the checkout counter, then ran to the back and stowed my stuff in my locker in the break room.

A few minutes later, I was hard at work finishing the window display. I pressed a set of floral window clings against the glass. Then, I set up book stands in a semi-circle with a gap at the back. I carefully arranged the books I'd selected yesterday, all of them featuring the same creature: griffins. Most were swoon-worthy romances, a few mysteries featuring a famous griffin-shifter detective, but I also had a scattering of historical and other non-fiction books.

"All about griffins," I said with a nod.

Then, I went back to the checkout counter and spent the next thirty minutes folding origami flowers. Thanks to the wonder of the internet, I was able to look up tutorials for a few different types of flowers. When I was done, I scattered them around the base of the bay window, leaving a small clear space in the center. Then I carefully carried Chrys over and set her down in the place of honor right in the center. It would have been better if I had real flowers to surround her with, but beggars couldn't be choosers.

Remembering something, I hurried back to the break room and rifled through the cupboards and drawers before finally finding what I wanted. Someone had left a medicine dosing cup here, and it had never been removed. After washing it thoroughly, I poured a little sugar water into it, then snagged a few berries and a mealworm. I carried the food back to Chrys and tucked them into her nest with her.

She chirped her thanks and immediately dipped her beak into the sugar water, letting me know that this batch was more satisfactory than what I'd given her back at our apartment.

I stroked her head with my fingertip. "Yeah, I know. This one doesn't have the medicine in it. Let me know if you start hurting again so I can give you something for it. Or if you're hungry, or just need a change of scenery. I've got to finish opening the store."

Chrys chirped in agreement and nuzzled me affectionately.

"Don't worry—I'll never be far."

I finished the rest of my opening chores quickly and unlocked the door right on time.

***

It was a busier morning than usual, mostly due to Chrys. I had several customers walk in and ask about her. Many were concerned about her bandages, and several wanted to pet her—they walked away disappointed. A few asked me for books about teacup griffins, and I had to admit that I didn't have any.

During a lull between customers, I looked up reference books for teacup griffins and was shocked by the sheer number. If I'd had any money in my account, I'd have ordered a few for myself. As it was, all I could do was note down the requests the customers made and pass them to Violet when she returned. I made a mental note to look some of these books up in the library tonight—with any luck, they'd have at least one.

"I guess being a rare creature means everyone wants to study you," I muttered to Chrys when I took a quick break to pet her.

She chirped in agreement and preened.

"Yeah, you are pretty special," I said before hurrying back to the counter to help another customer.

A few minutes later, the bell above the door jingled, and I

looked at the new customer, a greeting dying on my lips. Between his broad shoulders, black suit, sunglasses, and scowl, everything about him screamed danger. He was young and handsome, and seemed like he'd be right at home on the cover of a steamy romance novel—probably one of the mafia ones. I didn't know who he was, but he terrified me. A little voice in my head told me that if I caught his attention, my life would change forever. I desperately hoped he'd quickly find what he wanted and leave. Or better yet, turn around and leave right now.

To my horror, he did neither and came directly for me.

"Miss Jacobs, I presume?" His deep voice did nothing to reassure me.

I squeaked out an affirmation. He reached into his suit jacket and flashed a badge. I felt I should sigh in relief, but it just made me more nervous.

"Agent Stone. I'm here about the incident yesterday involving a teacup griffin. Would that be the one in the window?"

"Yes."

He took off his sunglasses and studied me with piercing amber eyes, eyes that made me want to run and hide. "Tell me, in your own words, what happened."

I nodded and scraped together what little courage I had left. "I came in yesterday morning at eight am, like usual. I found the window display completely trashed and everything in a pile on the floor. I heard a chirping sound and found Chrys buried under the debris. I called the South Phoenix Magical Veterinary Clinic, hopped on the next train and headed up there."

He frowned at me, eyes narrowed in disbelief. "Were there any signs of forced entry?"

"None that I saw at the time. Later though, I found that vent dangling." I motioned to the vent I'd fixed last night.

"I see. I also see that you've applied for financial aid to cover your *familiar's* medical expenses."

I nodded.

"Since you are unable to properly care for her, I will be taking her with me."

"What?" My heart stopped. I couldn't have heard him right. He couldn't take Chrys with him, could he? The vet had promised everything would be fine. I felt the walls start to close in on me. The thought of losing Chrys gutted me, even if I knew she'd be better off with someone else.

"As I'm sure you are aware, magical creatures do *not* form familiar bonds with *humans*. I find your entire story to be suspect. I will be taking the griffin with me, where she will get *proper* care. And I *will* be investigating you."

He turned and strode over to Chrys' window. In a fit of desperation, I darted out from behind the counter and grabbed his elbow. "No! Please, you can't!"

He spun towards me, his eyes flashing dangerously as he grabbed my wrist. Chrys shrieked in alarm. "Don't you dare presume to—"

I didn't hear the rest of what he said because, for the second time in less than twenty-four hours, the world fractured and slid away.

Images and feelings flashed through my mind faster than I

could make sense of them. Shadows, trees, feathers, danger, time running out.

Chapter 12

Miriam

REALITY WAS SLOW TO WELCOME ME BACK. Something poked my cheek repeatedly, and I opened my eyes to scold whoever it was. Instead of a person, I found Chrys kneading my cheek with her paws and purring. Everything hurt, and my head pounded like it was auditioning to be a percussion instrument.

"Huh. I didn't know griffins could purr."

"This kind of thing happen to you often?" a voice asked.

I turned my head towards the sound, only to find a pair of shiny black shoes inches from my nose. I looked up to find Agent Stone crouched beside me, a look resembling *concern* stamped on his face. Unlike Lucas, there was something calculating about his expression, as if that was how he knew he was *supposed* to look but had no practical experience with the emotion.

"Please," I said, covering Chrys with my hand, "you can't take her." I didn't know how she'd gotten there, but I wasn't letting her go without a fight.

He sighed. "It is against the law for SAID to remove

familiars from supernaturals without evidence of abuse or gross neglect."

I still had no idea if that meant I could keep Chrys. The bell above the door dinged.

"Miriam!" an elderly voice exclaimed. "Are you alright, dear? Was it another one of your seizures?"

This was a voice I welcomed, even if the owner of it was a bit too nosy for my liking.

"Hi, Mildred," I said. "Give me just a moment, and I'll be right there to help you."

I struggled to sit up, but Mildred waved me off, a mischievous glint in her eyes. "You'll do nothing of the sort, dear. You just sit back and let that handsome man take care of you."

Agent Stone "taking care" of me sounded far more ominous than Mildred had intended.

Everything ached, and I wanted nothing more than to lie down and take a nap. Still, I forced myself to my feet, ignoring Agent Stone's hand when he offered it. He'd treated me like dirt before, and I didn't trust his sudden change of heart. Chrys climbed up my face and made herself comfortable on top of my head.

"How frequently do you have these ... seizures?" he asked.

I folded my arms and scowled at him. "That is none of your business."

He scowled back. "Right before you fell, your familiar put up quite the racket. Has she done anything similar before other seizures?"

I thought back to last night when Chrys had started shrieking while I was on the ladder. I slowly nodded. "Yes, last night."

"She's probably alerting you. Next time, lie down. You fell and hit your head pretty hard on the floor."

I reached up to gently finger the goose egg growing on the back of my head. *No wonder my head hurts so much. Did he even try to catch me? He was right there!* The thought that he hadn't bothered to catch me was just another point in his minus column.

"Do you … see … anything during your seizures?"

I rolled my eyes. "Seizure symptoms vary depending on the area of brain affected. Symptoms can include visual, auditory, olfactory, tactile, gustatory, and even emotional hallucinations."

That was just a fancy way of saying that any sense could be tricked, depending on what area of the brain was hit.

"Fascinating. But that doesn't answer my question."

"Your question is none of your business."

"Are you taking seizure medication?"

"Again, that is none of your business."

His scowl deepened. "If you are, I suggest stopping—it's doing you more harm than good."

"Thank you for your expert medical advice. Will there be anything else today?" I gave him my best customer service smile. He might have had a point about my seizure medication—two seizures in less than a day hinted that it was losing efficacy, or I was building a tolerance. As long as I was taking it daily, my seizures were normally weeks apart. I froze as a horrible realization swept over me. In my rush to get out the door this morning, I had forgotten to take my medicine.

Agent Stone muttered something under his breath and stalked out.

***

Chrys chirped from the top of my head, and it took me a few minutes to figure out that she wanted to go back to her nest. She'd been up there the entire two hours since Agent Stone had left, save for a few minutes when I'd given her medicine. Several customers had gushed over her and asked how I'd managed to train her to do that. One uppity lady had looked down her nose and commented how unhygienic it was to have a bird in my hair and wondered what the world was coming to. I wished her a day as pleasant as herself—I'm not sure why she looked offended at that.

"Alright, I've got you."

I held my hand up, and she climbed onto my palm. I shuffled over to the window where her nest was and gently deposited her inside. She chirped at me again, demanding that I bring her with me back to the counter. I dutifully carried her back, then glanced at the clock for the billionth time.

"Is that thing broken? How can I still have five hours left?"

I sank onto the stool and rested my head on the counter, my stomach grumbling as I thought of the leftovers waiting for me in the fridge. Normally Violet was here, and we took turns taking a lunch break, but with her gone, I'd have to wait for a lull in customers so I could go back and sneak a few bites.

Chrys moaned and a sense of discomfort washed over me. I raised my head and looked at her in concern.

"Are you okay?" I asked, reaching out for her.

She pecked me sharply with her beak, and I quickly withdrew my hand. A few minutes later, Chrys stopped moaning, and the uncomfortable feeling passed. I raised an eyebrow as I looked at her. Her feathers and fur puffed up, and she looked at me with what I could only interpret as pride. She stood and moved to the side of her nest, giving me the incredible view of two dark blue eggs.

"Oh, Chrys, they're beautiful."

She chirped in agreement and settled back down on top of them. I stroked her gently with my fingertip, feeling awed that she shared such a special moment with me. I felt a stab of sorrow and grief that I knew was Chrys missing her mate.

"I'm sorry, love. We'll try to find him." I didn't know how, but we would.

Three pm rolled around, and I wanted to cry. I had never been so desperate for seven pm.

I closed my eyes for just a moment, breathing through a spike of pain. The bell jingled, signaling another customer, but I couldn't dredge the energy to greet them.

"Delivery for Miriam and Chrys."

I opened my eyes and found myself face-to-face with a potted plant with tall stalks of purple flowers.

"I'm Miriam," I said. *But who knows about Chrys?*

The delivery man moved the flowers to the side, and I was met with Lucas' smiling face. "I know," he said, then frowned. "Are you okay?"

I sniffed, my vision suddenly blurring with tears. I tried to tell him I was fine, but nothing came out. Next thing I knew, he was beside me, pulling me into his arms. It all came out in a flood of tears.

"I forgot to take my medicine this morning and had another seizure. Everything hurts, my head is killing me, and I need to eat, but the headache is making me nauseous. I can't call anyone to take over, and if I close the store early, my boss will fire me, and I really need this job."

Pull yourself together! You are a strong, independent woman, and you are not making a good impression. He's probably wondering who allowed you to live on your own.

As much as I wanted to prove that I was capable of handling my own problems, there was something *safe* about falling apart around Lucas. He'd seen me at my worst, and instead of running, he'd tucked me into bed and made me food.

Chapter 13

Lucas

CRAP, CRAP, CRAP, CRAP! She's crying! What do I do?! Okay, hold on, what does Azalea always say? That it's a compliment when women cry on your shoulder because it means you're safe to fall apart around. They know you'll help them pick up the pieces when they're done instead of stomping all over them.

It was a sweet sentiment but not particularly useful advice, aside from the *don't stomp on them* part. I still had no idea what I was supposed to do in this situation. I knew what I *wanted* to do, which was take Miriam back home and tuck her into bed, but something told me that forcing the issue was a bad idea.

"Women don't want you to solve their problems, they just want you to listen." That piece of advice came from my younger sister, Iris. That was a lesson she'd beaten into me, literally.

We stood there for a few minutes with her head tucked under my chin and her tears soaking my shirt. As I held Miriam, a customer walked up and quickly decided they were not, in fact, ready to check out yet.

"Sorry," Miriam said with a sniff. "It's been a rough day."

"Sounds like it," I replied, spying a box of tissues under the counter and passing them to her.

"Thanks." She grabbed a tissue and dabbed at her eyes and nose. "You don't happen to have any ibuprofen on you?"

"I might have some in the first aid kit in my car," I replied.

I pressed a kiss to her forehead and bolted out the door before I could think about my actions.

When I stepped back into the store, Miriam was busy helping a customer check out. I stood off to the side, waiting for her to finish. I passed her the medication, which she took with a grateful look.

"I brought some pastries too." I held up the box I'd left in the passenger seat on my first trip.

She gave me a watery smile. "You're a lifesaver."

I grinned. "I don't know if pastries have saved any lives before, but my mom would probably disagree with me."

She smiled tiredly and nibbled on the corner of the pastry.

I could tell when the medicine kicked in because she perked up and wolfed down the remaining treats. She still looked tired, but not like she was a breath from collapsing. I couldn't force her to go home and rest, but I could at least make her job easier, so I hung around the bookshop for the rest of her shift, running errands and helping out however I could. At one point, I kept an eye on the counter while Miriam ran to the break room to give Chrys medicine. Throughout the afternoon, I caught her sniffing the *Angelonia angustifolia* when she thought I wasn't looking—she even lifted Chrys up to them a few times after I confirmed they were insecticide-free.

"You didn't have to stay and help, but I'm grateful you did," she said as we closed up.

"My pleasure," I replied, forcing back the words I really wanted to say. "Mind if I walk you to your car?"

She shook her head. "I don't own a car. The bus stop's not too far from here."

It was my turn to shake my head. "I'll take you home."

She balked. "I can't let you do that—you've done so much already."

"Please. I want to," I replied softly.

She nodded and looked away, a blush creeping up her cheeks. I couldn't help grinning as I helped her into the car. After she buckled, I passed her Chrys, then put her backpack and the flowers in the back.

"Um, thanks for the flowers," Miriam said as I climbed into the driver's seat. "They're beautiful."

"They're *Angelonia angustifolia,* also known as Summer Snapdragon or Angel Flower."

"Oh."

Her blush was adorable and did funny things to my heart. I hadn't been able to fall back asleep after I received her text at midnight. When I finally gave up on sleep, I went up to my greenhouse and spent the rest of the night preparing a cutting and using magic to speed its rooting and growth. It took every scrap of patience I had to get through my classes today instead of rushing out to give it to her.

"Despite the name, it's not a snapdragon, rather a lookalike that thrives in the summer, hence the name. Unlike the color-rich palette of snapdragons, the *Angelonia angustifolia* comes primarily in pinks, purples, and whites. They have a long bloom season and the nectar-rich flowers attract all manner of pollinators, including hummingbirds. They're a hardy little shrub and do well either in the ground or in containers. They can survive periods of drought and need lots of sunlight. Though they thrive in areas of high humidity, supplemental watering can help them survive the desert heat." I stopped talking, realizing I'd lapsed into lecture mode. "Sorry, I guess you can take the professor out of the lecture hall, but you can't take the lecture hall out of the professor."

"I don't mind," she replied. "How frequently should I water it?"

I flashed her a grateful smile—she might not mind now, but she would one day. "When the first few inches of soil are dry, it's time to water again. Just stick your finger in the soil up to the second knuckle. If it feels dry, water it. If it feels moist, hold off."

She nodded, then leaned her head back against the headrest and closed her eyes. "Thanks for coming—I don't know how I would have made it through these last few hours without you."

Chrys trilled.

"Chrys agrees—you're pretty awesome."

I blushed all the way to the tips of my ears. I turned to ask her where she wanted to eat, but she was already asleep. I drove to her apartment in silence, taking the scenic route and making a quick pit stop at one of my favorite food trucks.

"Hey," I said, shaking her shoulder gently. "We're here."

She woke with a start and looked around in confusion for a

moment. "I just closed my eyes."

I grinned. "You've been asleep for twenty minutes. I would have let you keep sleeping, but I thought you might want some food." I held up the bag in my hand.

She sniffed the air. "Wow. That smells *really* good."

I nodded. "Best street tacos in Wellspring."

She gave me a wry grin. "You know that's not a very high bar."

I laughed. "Yeah, but these put most of the ones in Phoenix to shame too. It started with a pair of troll brothers selling tacos out of their backyard. When the city shut them down because of licensing issues, their customer base banded together and got them their own food truck and even helped them file all their paperwork."

"Nothing brings people together like good food."

"Because good food feeds the soul," I said, finishing the old gnomish saying as I helped her out of the car.

She yawned, covering her mouth. "When I was little, I always wished I'd been born a gnome."

I looked at her in surprise. It wasn't uncommon for humans and even other supernaturals to wish they'd been born different, but they usually wished they'd been born as dragon or griffin shifters, or elves, or even merfolk. A gnome, though, that was unusual.

"No offense to elves," she hurriedly added, then yawned. "I just think gnomes have it right—food's where it's at. Gnomish culture always seemed so … welcoming. Again, no offense to elves," she repeated, swaying slightly on her feet.

I grinned. "I'm half gnome—trust me, I'm not offended by anything you just said. Also, sometimes elves really suck. The gnomish side of my family never made me feel inferior for any reason—the same can't be said for my elven family."

"Oh," Miriam said, frowning slightly, "then your elven family is stupid, because we've already established that you're pretty much the best."

I laughed as I slipped an arm around her. I had a feeling Mom would love her. We walked up to her apartment together, and I was surprised at how natural it felt to have my arm around her like that.

Chapter 14

Miriam

WORK THE NEXT DAY WAS LONG AND UNEVENTFUL. Though unusual for a Friday, it was a welcome reprieve from the chaos of the two previous days. Unfortunately, the unusually slow morning meant I spent a lot of time alone with my thoughts. I spent all of my downtime between customers obsessing about and overthinking everything I'd said. I'd worried that having Lucas in my apartment was going to be awkward, but it wasn't—probably because I was too tired to *make* it awkward. But now that I was awake and alert, maybe it had been awkward, and I'd just been too tired to notice.

I can't believe I told him I wanted to be a gnome. Tired Miriam had no filter. At least he hadn't seemed to be offended by it. It probably helped that he was half gnome, so he'd taken it as a compliment … maybe. *Or maybe he was just being nice and thought I was really weird. Although, if that was the case, why did he confirm our date on Sunday? How will I know when he loses interest? Will he stop feeding me? The horror. I need to know more about gnomish culture … and probably a little about elves too.*

As if sensing my tumultuous thoughts, Chrys chirped reproachfully.

"Yeah, I know. You're absolutely right. Lucas would just *tell* me if he wasn't interested. Right?"

Chrys chirped again, and I stroked her head.

"What would I do without you? I'm still gonna do some research, though."

I hopped off my stool and headed over to our non-fiction section. We had a few books about the various supernatural cultures, and it wouldn't hurt to brush up on them. I selected a few that looked interesting and carried them back to the front desk. When I rounded the corner and saw who was waiting for me there, the hair on the back of my neck stood up, and my heart raced.

What's he *doing here? He didn't come to take Chrys, did he? Her eggs! He came for her eggs! Wait, does he know about them?*

I gripped the books tighter and slid around the other side of the desk, hoping to keep the solid chest-high wood between me and the heartless SAID agent. I pasted a customer service smile on my face, even though I felt like screaming and throwing things.

"Agent Stone, how may I be of assistance today?"

"Miriam, these are for you." He produced a stunning bouquet of ruby-red roses from seemingly nowhere and thrust them into my arms.

I grabbed them reflexively, my eyes narrowing in suspicion as alarm bells rang in my head. Chrys hissed, which was all the confirmation I needed.

"Why?" I demanded.

He flashed me a smile that would have turned any normal woman into a gooey puddle. Unfortunately for him, I wasn't a normal woman—I was a seething ball of anxiety, paranoia, and a dash of anger. A few flowers and a smoldering smile weren't enough to get me to let down my guard.

"I just wanted to apologize for yesterday. I know I came off a little strong—I was taken aback by my sudden, *intense* feelings for you, and reacted poorly."

Red flags were waltzing through my head. This stank more than a pile of fresh puppy mines.

"Let me make it up to you. I'll pick you up after work, take you out someplace fancy, dinner, dessert, the works." He winked, and my skin crawled.

Nope. Nope. Nope. Nope.

"Just to be clear, your visit here today is of a personal nature?" By now, my smile likely resembled a grimace.

He winked again. "Very personal."

"Good, then get out before I call the cops. And take your roses with you." I shoved them back at him, but he took a step back and held his hands up in surrender.

"Keep them." He gave me another smoldering smile. "I like a challenge."

I barely withheld a full-body shudder.

Thankfully, he left after his chilling response. I spent the rest of the afternoon looking up other job openings, even applying to a few, including one at the conservatory. If he thought I was a *challenge*, he'd just keep coming back. As a government agent, filing a restraining order wouldn't do much.

My thoughts spiraled, pulling me down, down, down, through an endless loop of ever-more horrifying outcomes. I even looked up one-way plane tickets, hoping if things went to pot, they did so between my paycheck depositing and needing to pay rent. I sincerely hoped it didn't come to that, because the thought of leaving made me sick.

A chirping by my elbow and the gentle brush of feathers pulled me out of my doomsday thoughts. I scooped Chrys into my hands and held her up to my face, gently bumping foreheads. I felt my thoughts settle, and I took a deep, calming breath.

"Thanks. What would I do without you?"

Chrys chirped.

"Yeah, probably." I gently deposited Chrys back in her nest, then leaned down and kissed her soft, feathery head. I glanced over at the roses and scowled. "What do you think we should do with those? I kinda just want to throw them away."

Chrys chirped.

I sighed. "I know—it's not the roses' fault he was a total creep. But what do I do with them? I'm not keeping them."

She tilted her head and chirped again.

"Good idea. The next dozen customers that purchase a romance book get a free long-stemmed rose."

I poked the roses with another scowl. *I always thought giving someone flowers was a romantic gesture—I didn't realize it could set off every alarm bell I have.* I thought about Lucas showing up yesterday with an entire potted plant and how it had made me feel safe and cherished. *It's not about the flowers at all, but the person giving them.*

Giving away the flowers turned out to be an inspired idea. A group of elderly women shuffled into the store shortly after that, and they all picked out one of our spiciest romance novels. As they belonged to the same book club and *always* picked out a spicy romance, I knew they knew exactly what they were getting themselves into. Plus, it was the second one in the series—the first one had been last week's pick. They all shuffled out of the store, gushing over their roses and new books.

Afterwards, I had three roses left. I gave one to a woman buying a regency romance novel, one to a high school student buying a copy of *Romeo & Juliet*, and the last one went to an adorable little girl, just because.

"What do you say to Miriam?" her dad asked, grabbing his bag of board books.

"Tate tou!" she whispered and then blew me a kiss.

I pretended to grab the kiss and pressed it to my heart. "You are very welcome. Enjoy those books!"

"Bye Wyss! Sowwy huwt!"

Chrys chirped and fluffed her feathers.

Things picked up after that, and I didn't have time to worry about Agent Stone's unsettling behavior.

Chapter 15

Lucas

THE INCESSANTLY-RINGING DOORBELL pulled me from the rabbit hole of research I'd been doing regarding teacup griffins and their habitats. One of the jungle biomes needed an overhaul, and I thought Chrys might enjoy a taste of home. I'd already drawn up a few plans, but I really wanted to see what kind of plants Chrys liked best before submitting any of them. Maybe I was getting ahead of myself, planning a garden for my not-quite girlfriend's familiar, but once the idea popped into my mind, it was impossible to get rid of.

"Alright, alright, I'm coming." I shuffled to the door, the ears of my fluffy bunny slippers flopping with every step.

I opened the door and stared in surprise at the last person I expected to drop in on me unannounced. I poked my head out the door and peered around him but saw no one else. I took a step back, then narrowed my eyes at him.

"Wait, let me guess. Someone mistook my *Magicus*

floribunda[1] for *Arcanus floribunda*[2], and you're here to make sure I'm not, in fact, growing illegal magical flowers."

"Good guess," Jason said, "but no. Are you going to let me in, or are you going to make me wait out here while you hide your arctic florid buses?"

My eye twitched, and I gritted my teeth, knowing he only said that for a reaction, but unable to stop myself from correcting him. *"Arcanus floribunda."* I stepped aside and held the door open for him. "Arctic florid buses. Who raised you? A savage?"

Jason laughed and sauntered into my living room, flopping down on the couch and making himself comfortable. "Hilarious. I'll tell Mother you said that."

"I meant your father."

"He'd take that as a compliment."

I shut the door, then sank into the armchair across from him and tried not to fidget. "Yeah, he would. Don't take this the wrong way, but why *are* you here? You don't normally just drop in on old friends. Also, can I get you some refreshments?"

Jason was an old college roommate, and even though we were friends, he rarely came by just to visit.

He shook his head and raked a hand through his hair. "It's a mess, Lucas, an absolute mess. There's this girl, and Father wants me to marry her, but I'm not attracted to her, not in the

---

[1] *Magicus floribunda*: Magic rose. Has a glittery sheen and is used in many potions.
[2] *Arcanus floribunda*: Arcane rose (has a habit of exploding if it's set on fire, or if it just gets too hot). Illegal to own in Arizona and many other hot climates.

slightest. I mean, she's pretty enough, but not my type. Also, I'm pretty sure she hates my guts. I tried giving her roses today, and she acted like I'd given her a bouquet of snakes."

"So, tell your father no."

"It's not that simple," he said, jumped to his feet, and began pacing. "If I don't marry her, or at least have some kind of claim on her before the other clans find out about her, it could be a disaster."

Claim? The Dark Ages are calling. They want their baloney back.

"I'm not even going to begin to try to understand griffin shifter politics. How does *she* feel about all of this?" He refused to look at me. "She doesn't know any of this, does she?" He shook his head. "So, all she knows is that some guy keeps hitting on her and won't take no for an answer?"

"So, you see why I need your help."

I shook my head. "I have no idea what you want me to do besides tell you to back off and leave the girl alone."

He gave me an incredulous look. "I need you to be my wingman. Talk me up, make me look good—help me get her to fall for me."

His plan had more holes than Swiss cheese and was twice as stinky.

"And do *you* plan on falling for *her*?"

He looked away guiltily.

"No. Absolutely not. I will not help you scam some woman."

He scowled at me. "You don't understand the stakes."

"Then explain them to me, because from what I see, you're going to trick her into falling in love with you, and then you'll get married. You'll be miserable from the start, and she'll be miserable as soon as she realizes that you never loved her. Then, either she'll leave you, or you'll be miserable together for the rest of your lives. And what about the whole 'griffins mate for life' thing?"

"I should have known you wouldn't get it. Thanks for nothing." He stormed out, slamming the door behind him.

I stared at the door for several minutes, utterly bewildered. That had to be the strangest conversation I'd ever had with Jason ... if it could even be called that. He'd had always been a bit of a player, but he'd always respected a 'no' when it was given. This, this wasn't Jason. Then it dawned on me. He wasn't asking me to be his wingman—he was asking me to run interference.

I hurried back to my office and spent the next five minutes searching for my phone. I finally found it posing as a bookmark in a text about a variety of magical sequoia that was facing extinction due to deforestation. It was a fascinating read, and I was dying to get my hands on a specimen and attempt to propagate it. But, first things first.

I opened the messaging app on my phone and quickly created a new group.

> **Me**: SOS. Jason needs an intervention. Everyone available come to my place ASAP.

Nolan: Is this about that TTRPG again? Come on let a man have his weird interests.

Me: What? I have no idea what you're talking about. Besides, I play with plants for a living. I'm the last person that should throw stones.

Nolan: Burn!

Nolan: Self-burn!

Sean: So, what IS this about?

Me: We need to stop Jason from making a BIG mistake. I can't explain over text—it's too bizarre.

Dylan: Working a case right now, but one of my leads is up your way. Be there tomorrow.

Nolan: Just spilled hot sauce on Melanie's favorite sweater. Need somewhere to lie low for a bit. If I'm not there in three hours, look for me in a ditch.

Dylan: I'm surprised you didn't blame it on Phil.

Nolan: That's a fantastic idea!

Me: No, it isn't. Familiars can communicate with their keepers, remember?

Nolan: Oh, right. Phil's a total narc.

Sean: Your sister is a saint for putting up with you.

Nolan: Truth.

Sean: I have a few things I need to wrap up at work, but I can be there in a few days.

I slipped my phone into my pocket and hurried to get ready for the guests who were about to descend on my space. I cleared a stack of textbooks and half-graded papers off the coffee table and piled them on my desk. Then I stripped the two guest beds of their sheets and threw them in the wash. But the most important task was grocery shopping.

***

Nolan was already lounging on my couch, his feet propped on the coffee table by the time I got back. I didn't bother asking how he'd gotten in—he'd long ago proved there was no lock that could keep him out.

"There's more in the trunk. Make yourself useful," I said, jerking my head towards the door.

He heaved a dramatic sigh as he stood. "Yes, Dad." He ducked as he stepped out the door so his antlers wouldn't scrape the lintel.

Nolan schlepped the groceries in while I put them away. By the time we were done, my pantry was full to bursting, and there was a little of everyone's favorites. I might have gone a bit overboard with the food, considering I had no idea how long any of them would be staying, but there was no way I would let any of my guests go hungry.

"Mmmm, Cinnamon Squares," Nolan said as he poured himself a bowl of the sugary cereal. "So, what's this about? Jason's the *last* person I'd imagine would need an intervention. I just saw him this morning—he was a little grumpy, but that's normal for him."

"You saw him this morning?"

Jason dropping in on two of his old friends in one day was unusual.

Nolan nodded and shoveled a large spoonful of cereal into his mouth. "It had something to do with one of his cases. Can't say more than that."

That made sense. With Jason in law enforcement and Nolan working at a pharmaceutical lab, he'd probably needed help identifying drugs found during a bust.

"And he seemed normal?"

Nolan shrugged. "A little agitated and impatient, but I gathered the case was time-sensitive. So, are you going to tell me what this is about or keep me in suspense?"

My phone rang, and I grinned at the name that popped up.

"Suspense," I said as I stepped into my bedroom to answer.

Chapter 16

Miriam

I TRUDGED UP THE STAIRS AFTER A LONG DAY AT WORK. These open-to-close shifts were killing me. Thankfully, Violet would be back in a few days, and I had both Sunday and Monday off. I had Chrys' follow-up vet appointment on Monday, but other than that, I planned to lounge around doing nothing. I just needed to make it through tomorrow. Saturday was our busiest day, and I was dreading it.

I slid my key into the lock and shuffled inside. I dropped my bag by the door and carried Chrys over to the counter, where I'd left her hummingbird feeder. I paused as I looked at it. *I could have sworn I'd left it on the other side of the counter.* I was a little paranoid and hadn't wanted it sitting right next to the stovetop, and yet, it was. I shook my head, pushed the feeder over to the fridge side, and set Chrys down in front of it.

I went about preparing Chrys a plate of mealworms and berries and couldn't shake the feeling that everything was just a little *off*. It wasn't anything major, just that several things weren't exactly as I remembered leaving them. The plates were pushed up against the side of the cupboard, which I didn't remember doing. Same with the cups, and the bowls were pushed to the back. *Wow, I really wasn't paying attention this morning, was I?* I shook the oddity off and put the plate with Chrys' food next to the feeder.

Then I grabbed myself a plate and scooped the last of Lucas' breakfast casserole onto it. It hadn't lasted nearly as long as I'd wanted it to, but it was hard to control myself when it was this delicious. Halfway through my dinner, I froze, the food turning to ash in my mouth. My bed was *rumpled.* I knew beyond a shadow of a doubt that I'd made it that morning. Not only was it unmade, but the pillows were in the wrong order.

Sensing my distress, Chrys chirped worriedly.

"It's fine—just keep eating."

I sidled over to the silverware drawer to grab the closest weapon, a paring knife. After that, I made a quick sweep of the apartment. Being roughly the size of a shoebox, it didn't take long. The only feasible hiding places were the pantry and bathroom, and both were thankfully empty of bogeymen. Unfortunately, my sweep revealed even more things that were just a little off.

Chrys chirped reproachfully.

"Yeah, I know. I should have left and called the cops—that was dumb of me," I said, "but I can't tell how they got in, or if they even took anything."

Chrys chirped again.

"I know—there's nothing here *worth* taking, but still. What are the cops going to do without evidence? The doors and windows were all locked. The only proof I have is that my bed is messy, and a few things are *slightly* out of place. They'd write it off as me being anxious or paranoid."

My skin crawled, and I rubbed my arms, but the feeling persisted. I tried to finish dinner, but the food had lost its flavor. I choked down two bites before giving up. Then I went around the apartment, ensuring that the door and windows were securely locked. I gave the windows a tug, just to be sure, then circled back to the kitchen. I picked my plate up, then immediately set it back down and checked the vents. Those were all secure too. I managed another bite of food before making another circuit of the apartment.

I gave up eating and tried to distract myself. My skin still crawled, so I threw on my comfiest sweater and curled up on the armchair with Chrys and a new library book. After the tenth time reading the same paragraph, I gave up. Reading had never failed to distract me before, but even my favorite thing in the world couldn't shake the feeling of dread that had settled over me. I needed something else to distract me from feeling like prey in my own home.

Before I knew what I was doing, my phone was pressed to my ear as it rang. I didn't even know who I'd called.

"Hey, Miriam," Lucas' warm voice greeted me.

"Hey, Lucas." I hesitated as I scrambled to think of what to say next. I didn't really want to tell him about the break-in because we barely knew each other. *Should I just talk about my day pre-break-in? Do I ask about his?*

"How are you doing?" he asked.

Like a dam breaking, everything flooded out. I glossed over the incident with the SAID agent, merely mentioning that a creep had hit on me at work.

"I'm sorry," I said, wiping tears from my eyes. "I didn't

mean to dump all of that on you—I was really just hoping for a distraction."

"I'm on my way."

It was incredible how just four words had the strength to lift the weight off my shoulders.

"Pack a bag—you can stay in my guest room tonight."

"No, you don't have to do that," I protested weakly. I couldn't impose on him like that, no matter how desperately I wanted to.

It shocked me how much I trusted this man I barely knew. I'd met him just a few days ago, and yet, in that time, he'd proved to be someone I could trust and rely on.

"Miriam, I won't force you to come with me, but I want to make sure you're somewhere you feel safe tonight, wherever that is. Just say the word, and I'll get you there, a friend's, a hotel, or with me."

I sobbed. How did he always know the right thing to say? In just a few sentences, he'd deftly taken charge of the situation while still giving me a choice and respecting my feelings. I wasn't used to this kind of consideration. Though my parents had always obsessed with my safety, they rarely bothered to consider how I would feel about their heavy-handed decision-making, and whenever I dared to contradict them, my feelings were always dismissed, as they *obviously* knew best.

"Could you stay on the phone until you get here?"

"I'd be happy to."

"Well, you know about my day. How was yours?" I couldn't begin to explain my desperate need to hear him talk. It didn't even matter what he was talking about—I just needed to hear his voice. As long as I was listening to him, I wouldn't spiral in my own thoughts.

I hurried around the apartment, stuffing clothing and other necessities into my backpack. While I frantically packed, Lucas told me about his day, which was mostly spent grading papers and drafting plans for a new exhibit at the conservatory. His excitement was contagious, and I desperately wanted to take a peek at those plans. Maybe if Lucas and I were still together, I'd get to go to the grand unveiling of the exhibit with him. For a moment, I let myself dream beyond my next paycheck.

Stop it, Miriam. One day soon, he's going to get tired of your seizures and all the baggage that comes with them, and he'll leave. Or worse, he'll start smothering. Just enjoy this while it lasts.

"I'm coming up the stairs, so I'm gonna hang up now."

The line went dead, and anxiety and doubt sliced through me. I rubbed my arms, hugging myself. *Am I overreacting? Maybe it's just a neighbor playing a prank on me.* My paranoia wasn't convinced. *Maybe a night away is what I need to clear my head and calm down. I'm sure in the morning I'll wake up and have a good laugh about this.*

A knock sounded at my door, and my heart skipped a beat, imagining a shadowy knife-wielding figure lurking outside.

"Stop. It's just Lucas," I scolded my over-active imagination. Still, I checked the peephole before opening the door.

"Hey," I said, torn between wanting to throw myself into his arms and wanting to appear like I was somewhat composed and in control. Instead, I did what I did best and made things awkward by staring at him.

Chapter 17

Lucas

THE DOOR SWUNG OPEN, and Miriam stood there, a panicked look in her eyes even as she squared her shoulders and greeted me with a soft, "Hey."

She was fighting for control and losing. I slowly reached up and rested my hands on her shoulders. Gently, I pulled her towards me, ready to stop the moment she resisted. She leaned forward and buried her face in my chest. A second later, her slender arms slipped around me and squeezed. I held her close, and we stood like that for a few minutes.

"Thanks for coming," she said into my shirt.

"Anytime," I replied, and I meant it. If I'd stopped to think about it, I might have been scared at how fast I was falling for this pretty, kind, intelligent woman. Just a few days, and she already had me wrapped around her finger, and I couldn't be happier. "Are you ready to go?"

She nodded. "Would you mind taking the backpack while I carry Chrys and the feeder?"

"I'd be happy to."

She passed me the backpack that had been sitting on her bed. I shouldered it while she scooped up Chrys and the feeder from off the counter. Looking around the tiny apartment, I couldn't tell that anything was out of place, but I also wasn't as intimately familiar with it as Miriam was. Regardless, whether someone broke in or not, it was clear Miriam didn't feel safe here.

I took the feeder from Miriam while she locked the door behind us. Her scary neighbor had come out during the few seconds we'd been inside her apartment.

"Hey Mike," Miriam said, giving her neighbor a polite smile.

"Miriam." He nodded at her. "Saw some miscreant lurking around here earlier. Scared him off, but best keep an eye out."

Beside me, Miriam stiffened. "Th-thanks. I'm gonna spend the night at Lucas'. L-let me know if you see anything suspicious."

He nodded again. "Will do." He turned to me. "Take care of our Miriam. Hurt her, and you're dead."

"Understood, sir." Half of me was terrified of this man, and the other half was grateful that Miriam had good neighbors looking out for her.

The drive to my house was quiet and dark, the sun having long since set. Miriam's furrowed brows and distant expression told me she was a million miles away. Halfway back, I reached over and grabbed her hand. I squeezed it gently and wondered what I could do or say to make things better.

She squeezed my hand back then looked at me. "Before you got there, I was trying to convince myself that it was just a prank one of my neighbors pulled, but after what Mike said ..."

I squeezed her hand again. "You're welcome to stay with me as long as you need."

She squeezed back. "Thank you. A night or two should be enough, though."

We drove for a few more minutes before turning onto the gravel road that led to my house. I lived on roughly two acres of land behind the conservatory that was only accessible via a glorified narrow gravel road. It was a minor miracle that I'd been able to get a place as close to the conservatory as I had. Too bad we couldn't see it in the dark—I bet Miriam would have loved it. *Maybe that will be our third date.*

As we bumped down the road, I became aware of just how much my car shook. *Maybe Briggs was right.* No sooner had the thought formed than my car let out a series of alarming bangs and coasted to a stop.

"I'm so sorry," Miriam said, shrinking in on herself.

I raised an eyebrow. "What for? My mechanic's been telling me for months that I need a new car—it's not your fault I've steadfastly ignored him."

"Yeah, but if it wasn't for me, you wouldn't be stranded in the middle of nowhere."

I smiled and leaned across the center console to kiss her cheek. "Despite what it looks like, this questionable road is just a long driveway. As soon as we turn the bend, you'll be able to see my porch lights."

"Do you want help pushing your car up to your house?"

I shook my head. "Nah. I'll just call a tow truck first thing in the morning."

Her brow furrowed, and she bit her lip. "Is it really okay to leave your car in the middle of the road overnight?"

I shrugged. "My house is the only thing down this road. Besides, what are they going to do? Steal it? Even if they scrapped it, they'd get maybe fifty bucks for it."

With tomorrow being Saturday, I didn't have work, so I'd hit up the local dealerships as soon as they opened. My biggest concern was how I'd make sure Miriam got to work.

Miriam and I walked down the dark drive, using our phones as flashlights. With my phone in one hand and the hummingbird feeder in the other, I wished I had a third hand so I could hold Miriam's, but then, she'd need a third hand too.

As promised, we rounded the bend, passing a stand of juniper trees, and my porch lights shone in the darkness.

Chrys chirped.

"Yeah, we're almost there," Miriam replied.

I smiled, amazed at how quickly she'd bonded with the minuscule griffin. She was amazing, yet she doubted her worth as a keeper.

We climbed the steps to the porch, and I opened the door for her, ushering her ahead of me. The front door opened directly into the living room, with the open-concept kitchen directly behind it and the dining room to the left of the kitchen.

"Wow, Lucas. Talk about a glow-up. You got pretty."

Miriam jumped, and Chrys shrieked at the jostling. I looked over at Nolan, who was sitting cross-legged on the table, eating cereal directly from the bag. I made a mental note to write his name on the bag later. He wore penguin pajamas and a mischievous smirk that promised trouble. *I forgot he was here. Wow, I'm a terrible friend.* I hadn't seen his car in the drive, so he must have moved it around to the side of the house.

"Nolan, I swear, if you scare my girlfriend away, I will never cook food for you again."

Too soon! Too soon! Please tell me that did not come out of my mouth.

That wiped the smirk right off his face. Coming from a gnome, that was a serious threat—it was as good as saying I would disown him as my friend. And I meant it. Nolan had a good heart but a tendency to trample across boundaries. It wasn't that he purposefully disrespected boundaries as that he tended not to recognize they were there in the first place.

Nolan held his cinnamon sugar-covered hand up. "I promise to be on my best behavior. Also, when did you get a girlfriend? And does she have a sister?"

Fudgesicles. I did say that with my outside voice.

"About five seconds ago, and no," Miriam replied.

I looked over at Miriam, trying to gauge her reaction, but her face was carefully blank. I couldn't help but feel like I'd jumped the gun by calling her my girlfriend, and now I'd messed everything up. I needed to talk to her and fix my mistake sooner rather than later.

"Miriam, this is Nolan. Nolan, this is Miriam." I hesitated, not sure how much Miriam wanted me to share about *why* she was crashing here. In the end, I decided to leave that up to her. "Miriam, your room's this way." I turned to go down the hall to the right.

"Shouldn't your girlfriend go in your room?" Nolan asked, digging into the cereal again.

"Nolan," I hissed as Miriam blushed scarlet.

"Right, right. Minding my business. But seriously, are you *sure* she's your girlfriend?"

"Nolan," I snapped.

Nolan wisely stuffed his face with cereal so he couldn't talk.

"I'm sorry," I apologized to Miriam. "He's got a good heart but a permanently broken filter."

Miriam nodded and silently followed me down the hall. My thoughts raced, trying to figure out which problem to address first. I'd made a mess of this and wasn't sure how to dig myself out. Nolan had already claimed the first guest bedroom, so I led her to the second one at the end of the hall. The bed was bare, so I put her backpack on the floor and pulled a spare set of linens from the dresser. *Thank goodness Mom told me to keep spares there—I forgot to switch the wash.*

We'd almost finished making the bed and I still hadn't figured out what to say.

"Your roommate seems nice," Miriam said as she stuffed a pillow into its case.

"Nolan? He's not ... my roommate, that is. He was, a while ago, but not anymore. But he is ... nice, that is." I groaned and facepalmed. "I'm making a muddle of this."

Chrys laughed at me from the top of the dresser. At least, that's what I assumed that sound meant.

"So, we were roommates back in college, and now we're friends. We were friends back then too, obviously."

Miriam stared at me, and I realized I still hadn't explained why Nolan was here, sitting on my table and eating my food.

"We're setting up an intervention for one of our other friends, and everyone's meeting here to discuss it. Nolan's just the first to arrive. The others won't get here until tomorrow or later."

She fiddled with the pillow in her arms. "You didn't mention other guests—I don't want to impose."

"Miriam," I said, "having you here will *never* be an imposition. I didn't tell you about them because—this is going to make me sound like a terrible person—I forgot about them. When you called, all I could think about was getting to you. Nolan was sitting at my table eating cereal when I left, and I'm pretty sure I didn't even say goodbye to him."

"But, won't they need this room?"

I shrugged. "I've got a comfortable couch and a couple air mattresses—they can deal for a few days. And if they really need a room, they can fight Nolan for it. As far as I'm concerned, this room is yours. If this makes you uncomfortable, let me know, and I'll take you to a hotel."

She shook her head. "No, this is fine. It's just for tonight anyway." She paused, then slowly smiled. "So … girlfriend?"

My face heated, and the tips of my ears burned. "If that's alright with you."

I'd known her for all of five minutes, but I was already convinced I wanted a real and meaningful relationship with her. Hopefully I hadn't torched my chances by scaring her off and proving what an awful friend I was.

"Yeah, I'd like that."

I grinned, my heart soaring. I leaned over and kissed her cheek. "I'll let you get settled in. I'll be in the kitchen when you're ready for a tour. The bathroom's across the hall, first door on the right, if you need it."

"And if I don't, it's on the left?"

I laughed. "Right."

Chapter 18

Miriam

LUCAS LEFT, AND I PUTZED AROUND THE ROOM for a few minutes while I sorted through my thoughts. If I'd known Lucas lived in the middle of nowhere, I probably wouldn't have agreed to come with him—I'd seen too many horror movies for that to seem like a good idea. Then again, Wellspring was technically a rural city, so a lot of the population lived on remote(ish) plots of land. I wasn't sure why I'd been picturing Lucas living in the suburbs when he needed space for all of the plants he undoubtedly had. *Maybe it was the car.* Thankfully, his house didn't scream 'axe murderer' as much as it screamed 'plant hoarder.'

I wasn't too thrilled that he had another house guest he hadn't warned me about. If I'd known he had other guests, I would have refused his offer. Then again, safety in numbers … maybe. He said he'd simply forgotten, but I wasn't sure what to make of that statement. Either he was so obsessed with me that nothing else mattered, or, like he'd said, he was a terrible friend. *Or maybe, when I called him, panicked, he panicked too.* Then he went and declared me his girlfriend. He was either a sweet guy or a potential stalker. *Then again, he did give me an out.*

And he blushed. Axe murderers don't blush ... do they?

Normally I had really good instincts when it came to people, but I was a little strung out from the stress of the last few days. A devastatingly handsome SAID agent had been flirting with me, and all I wanted to do was scale the nearest tree and hurl pinecones at him until he ran away. He left me feeling caged and defensive. Lucas was handsome too, but with him, I wanted to scale *him* and never let go. He also fed me, and if there was one thing that got me to let my guard down, it was food. I worried that my full belly was messing with my normally spot-on intuition.

I snorted. "I'm like a raccoon—feed me, and we can be friends. Or girlfriend, in this case," I turned to Chrys. "What do you think? Keeper or creeper?"

Chrys chirped and preened.

"Yeah, that's what I think too. Just wanted to make sure the food wasn't coloring my opinion."

I stroked her head gently, and she leaned in, purring. I melted. Purring teacup griffins were cuter than purring cats, hands down.

"You really like it here."

Chrys was giving off waves of contentment, like this was exactly where she wanted to be. A small, secret part of me agreed with her. I quietly filed that thought away to examine later.

"Do you want to stay here or take a tour of the house?"

She chirped and motioned towards the door with her head.

I chuckled. "As you wish."

I scooped up her bowl and headed out to the kitchen, admiring the gleaming hardwood floors as I went. I found Lucas in the kitchen, chopping vegetables and Nolan stealing them.

"If you wait five minutes, I'll have some dip ready," Lucas chided him gently, the corners of his mouth turned up in a smile.

I paused at the end of the hall, not wanting to ruin the moment. *How did I not notice his gnomish heritage?* Gnomes were never happier than when they were feeding people they loved. It also explained why he kept showing up with food.

"Is it that ranch dip you used to make?"

"Would I make anything else?"

"Score! Need me to grab anything for it?"

"A tub of sour cream, a brick of cream cheese, and a bottle of ranch powder."

Nolan turned to the fridge and began rooting around. After a minute, he shut the fridge, the sour cream, cream cheese, and a bottle of ranch in his arms. He deposited his haul on the island next to Lucas.

Lucas looked at the ranch dressing and chuckled. "Sorry, the ranch powder's in the pantry. Third shelf from the top on the left in the bin labeled 'seasoning mixes.' Leave the ranch bottle out, though—I'll need it in a few minutes."

"It's a little scary how you know exactly where it is," Nolan replied as he opened the pantry. "Woah! You can get dry ranch? Sick!"

I slipped over to the other side of the kitchen and put Chrys on a counter free of food. "Anything I can help with?" I asked.

Lucas flashed me a smile, and my heart stuttered. I made it

my personal goal to be the cause of that smile as often as possible.

"There's a segmented serving platter in the lower cupboard behind you. Mind getting it out and giving it a quick wash?"

"Sure thing."

It didn't take long for me to find the serving platter and wash it. Once it was clean and dry, Lucas loaded it up with the veggies he'd chopped. Then he dumped the cream cheese into a bowl and beat it with a hand mixer. Once it was smooth, he added the sour cream and ranch powder and mixed it together. I'd had sour cream and ranch dip before, but never with cream cheese.

"Ranch powder, huh," Nolan said, examining the bottle.

I watched in mild alarm as he tilted his head back and raised the bottle.

"Uh, I wouldn't ..."

Too late.

Nolan coughed and spewed ranch powder, a cloud of white dust shooting from his mouth. Luckily, he'd had enough presence of mind to turn away from the counter first. He bolted to the sink and stuck his head under the faucet. Lucas looked up from the dip he was mixing and gave the most long-suffering sigh I'd ever heard.

"Sorry, Dad," Nolan said sheepishly, dripping water all over the floor. "I thought that would taste better than it did."

Lucas looked at me. "Clearly our intelligence skipped a generation," he deadpanned.

"They say it's perfectly normal for toddlers to make messes

as they explore their world," I replied, struggling to keep a straight face. "I'm sure he'll grow out of it ... when he's ninety-two."

"See? Mom likes me ... hey, wait! Rude." Nolan pouted as he fished a rag out from under the sink and started cleaning up.

I laughed as I grabbed another rag and helped him. A few minutes later, all traces of Nolan's misadventure were gone, and Lucas had moved on to mixing up a yummy-looking chicken salad with ranch and avocado.

"Tour first or food first?" Lucas asked.

"Food, please," I answered, thinking mournfully of my unfinished dinner.

A few minutes later, the three of us and Chrys sat at the table with croissant sandwiches stuffed with delicious chicken salad, lettuce, and tomatoes. The veggie tray and dip sat on the table between us. Chrys had a selection of berries and a thimble of sugar water.

Lucas eyed Nolan. "Do you need a bib? I hear toddlers are messy."

I snorted, narrowly avoiding choking on my bite of sandwich.

"Rude," Nolan said as he threw a carrot at Lucas.

"They also have a penchant for throwing food," I added with a sage nod.

"I can't believe you two are ganging up on me," Nolan complained.

I looked at him with wide eyes and an innocent expression. "We're your parents—we have to show a united front."

Nolan gaped at me for a moment before sitting back in his chair and pouting.

I shook my head and looked at Lucas. "Threenagers."

Lucas lost it and had to excuse himself from the table while he regained his composure.

"Alright, I give up. I know when I'm beat," Nolan said, waving his napkin in surrender. "So, how did you two meet? Wait! Let me guess. One of your girlfriends dragged you to a lecture given by a hot professor with a shmexy voice. And it was love at first sight." He clasped his hands under his chin and batted his eyes.

I snickered. "No, but close. We met at the train station when I was taking Chrys to the vet. He invited me to a lecture he was giving, but I hadn't planned on going. Long story short, I ended up sitting front and center at the lecture, mostly thanks to a gremlin derailing my train. He asked me out for lunch after, and well …" I trailed off.

"You realized the eye candy had a heart of gold, and you'd be foolish to let him go?"

"Well, yes, but it's more than that," I said, playing with my cup as I tried to organize my thoughts. "He's fun to be around, but more importantly, he's *safe* to be around. Like, I know I can fall apart around him, and he'll hold me. Then, when I'm done breaking, he'll help me pick up the pieces and put myself back together. It seems crazy to feel that way about someone I just met, but I'd bet everything I have that it's true."

The scary thing was, I hadn't realized how strongly I felt that until the words came out of my mouth.

Chapter 19

Lucas

THE LOOK ON NOLAN'S FACE when Miriam called him a threenager was too much. I had to run to my room while I composed myself. When I finally got myself under control and opened my door to rejoin my guests, I caught the end of their conversation.

"You realized the eye candy had a heart of gold, and you'd be foolish to let him go?"

Eye candy? Seriously!? Maybe I should put dye in his shampoo. My face burned with embarrassment, but before I could do anything about it, Miriam's next words froze me in my tracks. I was a statue as words I wasn't meant to hear pierced my soul.

I backed into my room and quietly shut the door. Then I leaned against the doorframe and cried. Even after all those times hearing Azalea say it, I hadn't realized just how precious that trust was until Miriam. It took me another minute to compose myself.

I dried my tears and pulled my phone out.

Me: Thanks Zae. I owe you one.

Azalea: Yeah, you do.

Azalea: Why?

Jonas: Yeah, why? Why not owe me?

Iris: Or me?

Orchid: I'm feeling left out. Maybe we just say Lucas owes all of us.

Mom: Is this about your girl?

I groaned and ran my hand down my face. I'd sent that message to the family chat by mistake. And now the floodgates were open.

Orchid: Lucas has a girl?! SINCE WHEN?!?!?!?!

Jonas: I thought u were gay

Mom: If he was, I'd be asking about his boyfriend.

Iris: Yeah, since when? Why am I just now hearing about this?

Azalea: Yeah, why? And how serious is this?

Jonas: Do I need to come vet

her?

Me: You will stay as far away from her as possible.

Orchid: Oooooo VERY serious 😁 😁 when's the wedding?

Jonas: I'm offended

Mom: Spring weddings are nice.

Azalea: It's spring right now. You want him to wait a whole year?

Mom: Who says I want him to wait?

Me: Please stop planning my wedding to someone I met two days ago.

Iris: Only two days? I feel better now.

Dad: Sometimes that's all it takes. When you know, you know.

Orchid: Wedding colors?

Me: I sincerely regret opening this can of worms. I'm putting you all in time-out now.

Orchid: Eww! Not the underwear drawer!! 😨

That's not a bad idea. I turned the volume off and chucked my phone into the dresser.

***

"And this is my favorite room," I said as I paused on the landing outside my top-floor greenhouse.

"And here I thought it was the kitchen," Miriam teased, her brown eyes dancing.

"No, but that's a close second," I replied with a grin.

I opened the door for her then flicked the lights on. The awe on her face when she saw the rows and rows of plants made me giddy.

"Hey, Liza," she said, reaching out to brush the fern I'd put on the bench earlier today.

If Liza had been a cat, she would have purred.

Chrys had requested to be left in the room to sleep, and I couldn't help but feel that the teacup griffin had ulterior motives. I'd have to get her some fresh berries in thanks.

The greenhouse was bursting with plant life, the energy so vibrant the air practically hummed with it. I'd been in many greenhouses before, but I not-so-secretly thought mine was the best. Every time I was here, I could feel all my stress just drop away. I gave Miriam a thorough tour, introducing her to every plant. I showed her my successes, including a gorgeous dwarf hibiscus that made her eyes light up, my towering *Vanilla planifolia*[3] that yielded the most fragrant and flavorful bean pods (it was a point of pride that Mom now refused to source her vanilla beans from anyone but me), and the *Tacca chantrieri*[4], the *Impatiens psittacina*[5], and the *Cosmos atrosanguineus*[6].

"It smells like chocolate!" she exclaimed.

I grinned. "Its common name is 'chocolate cosmos.'"

"It looks like chocolate and smells like chocolate. Next, you're going to tell me it tastes like chocolate."

I shook my head. "I don't advise eating them. They're not toxic, but they're also not edible. I once gave my mom a bouquet with several chocolate cosmos in it. She put it on the kitchen counter—you should have seen my siblings wandering around the kitchen looking for the chocolate they thought she was hiding. My brother, Jonas, even went so far as to check the dishwasher. His reasoning was that it was the last place anyone would think to look."

Miriam laughed, her whole face lighting up. I plucked one of the flowers, sending a tendril of magic into the stem, severing it neatly. I tucked the velvety flower behind her ear, brushing her cheek with my thumb. Her breath hitched, and she looked at me with wide, expressive eyes.

"You make the flowers beautiful," I whispered. I'd never thought that about anyone before, but compared to Miriam,

---

[3] *Vanilla planifolia:* the vanilla bean orchid. Vanilla extract is made from the bean pods.
[4] *Tacca chantrieri:* Black bat flower
[5] *Impatiens psittacina:* Parrot flower
[6] *Cosmos atrosanguineus:* Chocolate cosmos

flowers were dull and lifeless things.

She blushed and looked away. With supreme effort, I dropped my hand and stepped back. Though I wanted nothing more in the moment than to kiss her senseless, I didn't want to rush things and scare her off. I'd already made the faux pas of calling her my girlfriend after only knowing her a few days. I didn't want to pressure her into giving me something she wasn't ready to give, even if it was "just a kiss."

We moved on to the edible garden, and she gaped at the planter box bursting with ripe strawberries. I plucked a few and passed them to her. Her exclamations of delight made my heart soar.

"These are the *best* strawberries I've ever had!" She looked around, taking in the entire greenhouse and me with an appreciative gaze. "Everything here is amazing—how do you manage it all on top of being a professor?"

I shrugged awkwardly. The truth was, I didn't know. Ever since moving here, my magic had grown stronger. It was such a gradual increase that I hadn't noticed it at first. It wasn't until Dad made a comment about my wildly successful new cultivars that I registered that anything had changed. While I'd inherited some nature magic from Dad, I'd always considered myself the weakest of my siblings. But my ability to create new and successful cultivars and propagate rare and difficult-to-grow specimens now far outpaced my siblings.

Once, after seeing my greenhouse for himself, Dad joked that he should turn the family business over to me and take an early retirement. I knew he meant it as a compliment, but the thought of leaving here had nearly sent me into a panic attack. Dad hadn't noticed, but Mom had. She'd simply smiled and patted my cheek, saying she'd always known that when I found my place, I'd sink my roots deep. Of course, that wouldn't stop her from asking me to come visit all the time.

"You're pretty amazing, Lucas—I hope you know that," Miriam said.

I had nothing to say to that because most of the time, I felt like a fraud, like one day someone would look at me and say, "Hey, wait a minute ... does this guy *really* know what he's talking about?"

Next thing I knew, Miriam's arms were wrapped around me, her head resting on my chest. "You are the kindest, most caring, most intelligent person I know. And I defy anybody to say differently."

I held her close and wished for time to stop.

Chapter 20

Miriam

NORMALLY IT WOULD TAKE ME A LONG TIME to fall asleep in unfamiliar places, but the ridiculously comfortable mattress and full belly, combined with sheer exhaustion, conspired to pull me under the moment my eyes closed. Despite a comfortable bed and a full belly, my dreams were troubled.

I ran down a narrow gravel path, shadows reaching out to grab me. I dodged their grasping tendrils, knowing that if I stopped, I'd be caught. I didn't know what chased me, only that it filled me with dread. Chrys sat in her bowl, urging me on. My heart pounded loudly in my ears as I gasped for breath. The path stretched endlessly before me. No matter how fast I ran, the end was never any closer. Then I saw him. Lucas stood at the end of the path, his arms stretched out towards me. If I could just reach him, I'd be safe.

I ran and ran, but the distance between us grew. I tripped and fell, sliding on the gravel. Dozens of tiny rocks bit into my skin, and I sobbed as I scrambled to my feet.

Something cold and clammy grabbed my ankle, pulling me

down as it dragged me back. I clawed at the path, scrambling for purchase as a sick feeling rose in my throat. I risked a look over my shoulder, and my breath froze in my lungs. Formless darkness bubbled and writhed behind me, tentacles snaking out and consuming everything in its path. One dark tentacle wrapped around my ankle, drawing me in.

I screamed.

"Miriam! Miriam!" the voice seemed to come from miles away. I was afraid to look, but it was persistent.

I gasped and opened my eyes, feeling like I was resurfacing after a long time underwater. My heart thundered as I looked around wildly. I was in bed, but I wasn't alone. Nolan stood in the doorway, and Lucas sat beside me. Lucas looked concerned, and Nolan looked positively freaked out.

I sat up and practically threw myself at Lucas. I wrapped my arms around him, shaking so hard I thought I'd fall apart. The nightmare was over, but Lucas was still my safety.

"It was just a dream. Just a dream. Just a dream," I said into his chest. If I repeated it enough, maybe the terror would leave. As I clung to him, the details began slipping away, leaving only a sense of dread.

"It's okay. I'm here," Lucas whispered, holding me close.

Chrys chirped and nuzzled my neck in agreement.

It was a long time before I let go.

"I'm sorry," I said when I finally pulled away. "I didn't mean to wake you up."

"Don't worry about that," Lucas said, then pressed a kiss to my forehead. "Do you want to talk about it?"

I shook my head—I couldn't tell him about it even if I wanted to. "Nah—it was just a nightmare. Don't worry about it."

Lucas frowned but didn't argue.

"Really, I'm fine. It was probably just stress related. Go back to bed."

With visible effort, Lucas refrained from arguing, but the concern never left his eyes. "If you're sure. If I'm not up when you need to leave, just knock on my door. Nolan's letting me borrow his car."

I agreed, and Lucas left. Despite my words to him, I couldn't shake the feeling that my nightmare *was* something to worry about. If only I could remember it.

***

Saturday was always our busiest day. A few hours after opening, and I was already feeling run off my feet. It didn't help that I hadn't slept well after my nightmare. The only thing keeping me going right now was the thought of the lunch Lucas had packed me.

The thought of the delicious food slightly mollified my frustration with him for keeping an important piece of information from me. I still couldn't believe he lived next to the conservatory and hadn't bothered telling me.

There was a lull between customers, and I sat down, more than ready to take a quick breather. The bell above the door chimed, and my heart plummeted to my toes when I saw who it was. *When will he get the hint?* Dealing with the SAID agent was the *last* thing I wanted to do today, but it seemed like the universe wasn't interested in granting my wishes. If the package of chocolates under his arm was any indication, he wasn't here for business reasons.

I reflexively grabbed Chrys' bowl and held her close, standing as far back from the counter as I could get. I didn't know what it was about this man that made me want to run screaming, but I didn't trust him.

"Miriam," he greeted me, practically purring as he looked me up and down, "you look nice today."

He put the chocolates on the counter and leaned against it as he continued to stare at me. His look made me feel icky, and I desperately wanted to hop in the shower and scrub his gaze off. Chrys hissed at him.

"Agent Stone," I replied coldly, "what can I do for you today?"

He winked at me. "It's more about what *I* can do for *you*. Tell me when you get off, and I'll be here to pick you up for dinner, maybe some dancing after."

Where in the world would we go dancing in Wellspring?

"I'm not interested."

"If you give me a chance, I can fix that."

"Sir, I have a boyfriend."

He winked at me again. "He doesn't need to know."

Silent alarms were blaring in my head.

"Sir, if you have no *business* to discuss with me, then I'll have to ask you to leave."

"I would love to discuss *business* with—"

THUD! His face slammed into the counter, held in place by another massive hand.

I looked at my rescuer in awe. Heavily muscled and towering over even the tall Agent Stone, he was *built*. Even his perfectly tailored suit couldn't hide his muscles. Patches of scales ran across his hands and face, and his slit-pupiled eyes flicked towards me, assessing me. *A dragon shifter.* I'd never seen one before, but I was absolutely certain that's what he was. He turned his attention back to Agent Stone.

"The lady said 'no.' You're going to take that answer and *leave*. Nod if you understand."

Agent Stone nodded, and the dragon scraped him off the counter before frog-marching him out the door. My rescuer waited outside while the SAID agent beat a hasty retreat.

"I'm going to get in so much trouble for that," I muttered.

I wrinkled my nose when I noticed that my unwelcome suitor had left a little spittle on the counter. I put Chrys back down and grabbed a squirt bottle and rag from underneath. Spray. Wipe. Spray. Wipe. Spray. Wipe. Spray. Wipe.

"I think you've cleaned off every trace of him," a deep voice said.

I jumped back with a shriek. The dragon shifter stood in front of the counter, staring at me solemnly. *How can someone so large be so quiet?*

"I ... uh ... not *every* trace." I nodded at the chocolates still sitting there. "I don't suppose you want some fancy chocolate?"

He glanced down at them. "They're his?"

I nodded.

"Then I have no problems taking his stuff. But first, I am here on business." He flashed me his badge. "Agent Blazewing. You would be Miriam Jones, correct?"

I blinked. *Another SAID agent? What cosmic force did I upset? Whatever I did, I'm very, very sorry.* I reflexively grabbed Chrys and pulled her close to me again.

He raised an eyebrow. "I'm not here to take your familiar. I'm investigating a series of animal smugglings—magical animals, to be specific. I have reason to believe your teacup griffin was part of the latest shipment before she managed to escape. Can you tell me how you found …" he paused and checked his notes, "Chrys?"

I took a deep breath. Magical animal smuggling was bad, but at least he wasn't accusing me, and as a bonus, he was even remaining professional. I felt a flicker of hope—maybe he could help locate Chrys' mate. I went over the story again, and Agent Blazewing listened without a word.

"Would you point out the vent you think she came through?" he asked when I was finished.

I motioned to the vent by the window display, and he went over to stand under it.

"I'm going to need to look in it," he said after a minute.

I ran to the storage closet and grabbed the ladder and screwdriver. If a SAID agent wanted to poke around the vents, I wasn't going to stop them. As long as he didn't damage anything, I didn't care.

The Teacup Griffin

He examined the vent for a couple minutes, and I went back to the counter to help a few customers. As I finished ringing up the second one, he screwed the vent cover back on. He had a good poker face, I'd give him that. I couldn't glean any clues from his face.

"I don't suppose you and Chrys have bonded enough for her to tell you where she was before she came here?"

I shrugged and looked down at Chrys and repeated the question. She chirped and trilled a long answer, finishing by jabbing her beak in the air several times.

"She says no. It was windy and dark when she escaped from the 'large moving nest.' She got turned around and could barely tell up from down when she got tangled in the 'fireflies.' She also says that if she finds whoever has her mate, she will stab them in the eyes ... repeatedly, and a few other things I'm not sure how to translate."

Agent Blazewing chuckled and held out a finger for Chrys to sniff. "A mighty little fighter—I'll keep that in mind." Chrys bowed her head, and he gently stroked her neck. "I'll do everything in my power to bring your mate back to you."

My heart melted a little at how gentle the big, deadly dragon shifter was being with something he could squash like a bug.

Chrys shrieked, and a strange pressure built in my chest.

"Persimmon!" I blurted out, the pressure immediately easing. "You have to find them. There's not much time. You have to find persimmon."

I stared at the agent, shocked at the nonsense that had just come out of my mouth.

"Per…simmon?"

"I … I have no idea. I don't know why I just …" I trailed off, mortified. *What was that about? Persimmon? Really?*

"Persimmon," he mused, looking at me speculatively.

I shrugged, wishing I could crawl into a hole or that a customer would have a sudden book-related emergency for me. Or any emergency that didn't involve bodily fluids.

He reached into his pocket and withdrew a business card. He passed it over to me. "If you think of anything else, or Chrys remembers anything, call me."

I took the card with a silent nod, and he left.

I blew out a long breath. "Persimmon? Really?" I looked at Chrys. "I'm officially losing it."

Chrys chirped, scolding me.

"Time sneeze? It's time to sneeze? You need to sneeze? I need to sneeze?" I looked at Chrys, hoping for more guidance on what she'd meant. "My brain sneezed? Anything at all to do with sneezes?"

She gave me an exasperated look, telling me I was nowhere close.

"Yeah, I got nothing." I shrugged. "It's not like translating for you is an exact science."

Growing up, I'd always thought familiars spoke to their keepers with actual words. The truth was a lot more complicated. Sometimes it was impressions, sometimes it was like the meaning was dumped directly into my brain, and other times, it was a bit like trying to understand toddlerese.

Chapter 21

Lucas

I STOOD IN THE DEALERSHIP PARKING LOT, feeling small and lost as I watched Nolan drive away. My old car had already been towed to the junkyard, and it wasn't coming back. I kind of wanted to point to a car at random and be done with it, but I'd been making do with my rundown car for years. If I was going to get a new one, I should at least make sure it fit my needs.

At the top of that list was better suspension—I was tired of feeling every bump in the very bumpy roads I frequently drove on. Also, four-wheel drive and decent trunk space for the plants I frequently had to haul. I'd been making do by renting a truck from the local home improvement store every time I needed it. Maybe it was time to get one for myself. I eyed the behemoths across the lot.

Never thought of myself as a truck guy. I can't deny it'd be nice to not have to rent a truck every time I needed to haul some trees. But I'm still not sold on needing something so massive.

"Good morning, sir! Anything catch your eye?" a voice said.

I jumped, startled. While I'd been lost in thought, a sales rep had snuck up on me.

"A new car. Well, not a car—I need something a little bigger. I need to be able to haul stuff. Plants … mostly small, but sometimes large. Trees. Not large ones, small ones, but too big for a car. And dirt—I move a lot of dirt."

I just about turned around and sprinted out of there. Anyone who said I'd outgrow my awkward phase lost that bet. To his credit, the salesman hardly blinked.

"My name's David, and I'm more than happy to help you out this morning. Are you leaning more towards a truck or SUV?"

"Yes." I grimaced—that wasn't what he meant.

"And do you have a car to trade in?"

I shook my head.

"Then why don't we start over here with our trucks?"

I walked around the truck, sat in the driver's seat, and nearly told the sales rep I'd take it just to be done with the experience, then I realized something. I looked over my shoulder at the back of the cab.

"There's nowhere for car seats," I said. *Why did I say that? Why didn't I just say there wasn't a second row? Why am I like this?*

"Ah, car seats," David said with a sage nod. "In that case, the crew cabs are going to be a safer bet. Most of them have four full-size doors, which is very useful when dealing with bulky car seats."

I hopped out of the first truck. "You sound like you're

talking from experience."

He chuckled. "I am. Got three kids myself. Let me tell ya, babies are cute, but I'm glad the car seat days are behind me. How many you got?"

"None yet. Maybe someday ... hopefully. There's this girl ..." *Somebody take this shovel from me, so I stop digging.*

David was *good*—he didn't even twitch. "No harm in planning for the future."

Car seats. Maybe Dad was right. I'm so glad my family's not here to see this—I'd never live it down.

A few hours and several test drives later, I drove off the lot, the poorer owner of a new-to-me truck that somehow managed to feel both excessive and not quite enough at the same time. Half of me thought I should have just gotten another sensible compact car, but the other half of me knew my needs had outgrown that car.

I drove back home, surprised at how smooth the trip down my gravel driveway was. For once, I didn't feel like my teeth were going to rattle out of my head.

"Yeah, I should have done this ages ago," I reluctantly admitted to myself.

I parked behind an unfamiliar SUV. *Dylan must have gotten in.* I made a mental note to pull a few steaks out and get them marinating for lunch. Thinking of lunch reminded me of the one I packed Miriam this morning. I felt a stab of regret at the forethought. If I hadn't packed her lunch, I'd have an excuse to swing by the shop and see her.

"Get it together, Lucas. You'll see her tonight."

I let myself in and found a burly dragon shifter sitting at my kitchen table, a laptop in front of him, and a fancy joystick in his hand. It was undoubtedly an expensive piece of government property, but it looked like a child's toy in his large hands. The furrowed brows and intense look of concentration told me I'd best not interrupt. A fancy heart-shaped box of chocolate sat on the table next to him. From the looks of it, he'd already eaten half the package. I wrinkled my nose in disgust—the wrapping was better than the product.

I hung my keys on the hook by the door and headed to the pantry. *What spices does Dylan like best on his steak? And where's Nolan? Normally he'd be bugging Dylan for a chance to use his fancy gadgets. Oh, ginger marinade and cracked pepper.*

I opened the pantry to grab the pepper grinder, even though I wouldn't need it for a while.

"Oh, there you are."

One of Nolan's hands was tied to a support pillar, and the other was elbow-deep in a bag of chips.

"You bugged Dylan too much again?"

He nodded, not looking the least bit repentant. He could have untied himself any time he wanted but had likely figured it was safer for him to hide out in the pantry. I rolled my eyes and grabbed the pepper grinder from the spice rack.

"Could I get a cold soda?"

I shook my head. "No. Drink a warm one. Consider it punishment for irritating one of my guests."

He pouted. "But I'm a guest too!"

"Yes, that's why you still get a soda ... just a warm one."

He sighed dramatically. "Fine. I guess that's fair. How'd car shopping go?"

I shrugged. "Fine. Got a truck. No, you can't take it for a spin."

He pouted again. "You truck people are so over-protective of your shiny toys."

I raised an eyebrow. "I think that has less to do with the toy and more to do with the person playing with them."

I closed the door, cutting him off mid-protest.

There was no fresh ginger in my fridge, so I headed upstairs to my greenhouse. I paused by the dwarf variety of hibiscus I'd cultivated, remembering how Miriam had gushed over it last night. Unlike other varieties, this was a true dwarf, topping out at four feet without the use of a growth regulator. The flowers had a deep blue center that transitioned into purple, then pink, and finally yellow along the edges. It had taken me years to perfect this cultivar, but it was worth it, not only for the numerous awards it had won, but also for the simple satisfaction of having done it. *That, and Miriam's face when she saw it last night.*

I moved a few rows over to my edible garden section and quickly located the ginger. I sunk my fingers into the dirt and grasped a handful of the roots. Sending my magic into the plant, I severed the chunk I needed. I pulled the thick root out and shook off the damp soil.

A few minutes later, I had the ginger washed and peeled. It might have been cheating, but my elf magic made peeling fruits and vegetables a breeze. I loaded the ginger into the blender with some water and let it puree. *I wonder how Miriam likes her steak.* After pouring the ginger slush over the steaks, I put the lid back on the dish and popped it back into the fridge to marinate for a couple hours. Then I picked up the blender to take it to the sink.

"That's it! Persimmon Lane!" Dylan shouted. "I could kiss her!"

I jumped, and the blender slipped from my grasp, landing on the floor and shattering into a hundred pieces. I glared at my dragon shifter friend. The blender, like most of my kitchen appliances, had been a gift from my family when I started college.

"Sorry," Dylan said as he frantically gathered his stuff. "I'll replace it. Send me the details, but I gotta go—now. Be back … sometime."

I felt like saluting as he rushed out the door.

"Is it safe to come out now?" Nolan asked, peeking out the pantry door, cheese powder coating his face.

"Yeah. The big, bad, scary dragon is gone."

And so is my blender. I briefly considered pulling the steaks out and marinating them in ketchup instead but ultimately decided I couldn't commit that kind of blasphemy no matter how peeved I was at Dylan. I'd settle for only giving him water to drink while he was here, even though I had plenty of his favorite energy drink on hand. *That'll teach him.*

I made Nolan wash his face in the guest bathroom while I swept up the glass shards. Then I pulled my phone out.

> **Me:** What's a good blender? I need to replace mine.
>
> **Mom:** I know just the one! We can put it on your wedding registry.
>
> **Me:** Mom
>
> **Mom:** Lucas
>
> **Me:** We just started dating. Stop planning our wedding.

Never mind the fact that I was already picturing our future children, not that I would ever breathe a word of that to Mom.

> **Me:** Mine broke. I really need a replacement.
>
> **Mom:** Do not take her down to the courthouse! No matter how desperate you are for a new blender! She deserves better than that!
>
> **Me:** I'll just look it up.
>
> **Mom:** Okay, but if you decide to elope, at least give us a video call so we can see!

Face burning, I shoved my phone back into my pocket.

"You okay there?" Nolan asked as he poked my cheek.

"You're a little red."

I batted his hand away. "I'm going for a drive."

"Awesome! I'll get the snacks!"

My protests fell on deaf ears.

Chapter 22

Miriam

I WAS SNEAKILY TRYING TO EAT MY LUNCH at the counter while keeping an eye on the busy store. Violet didn't like anyone eating on the floor, but she also didn't want the shop unattended, especially not on a Saturday. I figured eating at checkout was the lesser of the two evils.

It took all my willpower not to inhale it. Lucas had made me a chicken teriyaki wrap stuffed with lettuce and a host of fresh veggies, all of it seasoned and sauced to perfection. I could die happy after eating this wrap. I closed my eyes as I savored it.

"Yeah, his food makes me feel like that too," a voice said.

I opened my eyes to find Nolan standing in front of me, grinning goofily.

Chrys chirped in greeting, and Nolan gently stroked her head.

"Where did you come from?" I demanded—I hadn't even heard the bell jingle.

"You see, when a man and a woman—"

I slapped my hand over his mouth in mortification. "Not what I meant," I hissed.

"Good, 'cause I'm pretty sure one of your books would explain it better than I could," Nolan said, the sound muffled by my hand.

"I don't even want to know what he said."

I looked past Nolan to see Lucas approaching the counter, a book in his hand.

"Hey, handsome," I said, the words slipping out before they'd fully formed in my brain.

He grinned, his eyes crinkled as his whole face lit up. "Hello, beautiful."

A shiver zipped down my spine, and I started devising ways to get him to say that more, preferably every time he saw me.

"How's your day going?"

Somehow, I managed to scrape myself together enough to respond. "Better, now." *Now that you're here. Wow, I've been reading too many romance novels—I'm turning into a complete sap.*

"Rough morning?"

I rolled my eyes. "Mostly fine, except for this one jerk who can't seem to take 'no' for an answer."

I didn't miss the worried expression that flitted across Lucas' face. I wanted to downplay it, tell him that everything was fine, but the more I thought about it, the more it bothered me. I'd always been a good judge of character, and something was telling me that Agent Stone didn't have a sincere interest in me. The man was an official government agent. If it got bad, it had the potential to get *really* bad.

"It turned out fine though—a nice dragon shifter chucked him out of the store for me."

"Do you want me to stay?"

I shook my head. "No, thank you though. I don't think he'll be back today."

"If you're sure..." I nodded. "I'll pick you up when you get off tonight. You can stay the night again, if you want."

I smiled. "I'd appreciate it. Thanks."

I was looking forward to having a day off, and even more, I was looking forward to spending it with Lucas. We had a date tomorrow, but I couldn't remember what we'd planned on doing. It didn't really matter though, as long as it was with Lucas.

As if reading my thoughts, Lucas smiled down at me, his eyes crinkling. "I'm looking forward to our date tomorrow."

A kaleidoscope of butterflies took up residence in my stomach, and I'm sure my grin looked as sappy as it felt.

"Me too."

Chrys chirped and trilled, fluffing her feathers and bobbing her head.

"Chrys says she's looking forward to the date too."

Lucas chuckled, the sound sending my butterflies into a tizzy. "I'll try not to disappoint."

I don't think you could, even if you tried.

Lucas bought his book, and he and Nolan left. For the rest of my shift, time passed strangely—sometimes leaping forward in great bounds, and other times, the minutes stretched into eternity.

Like she had been the last few days, Chrys was a big hit, with so many people asking if they could take pictures of her. A few customers even came in specifically for Chrys, showing me where she was trending on social media.

"Look at that, Chrys," I said as I passed a young woman's phone back to her, "you're famous."

From what I saw, there were a lot of questions on the store's page about Chrys and her bandages. A few irate people were even threatening to report Chrys' abuse to SAID. I'd need to make a post regarding her sorry state so people would stop thinking she was in danger. While I didn't have admin access to the store's page, I could at least tag it from my personal account. I made a mental note to do that tonight before bed.

Finally, the end of my shift arrived, and I flipped the sign to 'Closed' as I ushered out the last customer. I quietly turned the lock behind them—no need to tempt fate to send someone who couldn't read a sign into a bookstore. Now, all I had to do was vacuum, straighten the books, reconcile the register, and a few other things.

I was finishing up vacuuming when my phone buzzed with a notification.

Lucas: Almost there.

I grinned and slipped my phone back into my pocket. A couple minutes later, there was a knock on the door. Figuring it was Lucas, I hurried over to let him in. I realized my mistake as I turned the lock. The man lunged through the door, grabbing my wrist and hauling me out as Chrys shrieked. I dug my feet in and wrapped my free arm around the door frame. Pressure built in my chest as adrenaline flooded my system.

"Let me go!" I screamed. "HELP! LUCAS!!"

The man clamped a hand over my mouth and wrapped his other arm around my waist, lifting my feet off the ground. I elbowed his stomach with all my might while kicking him but only succeeded in making him grunt. The pressure in my chest continued to build, then the world tilted, fracturing into a hundred pieces.

I was running from the encroaching darkness, gravel crunching under my feet. Fear flooded me, but if I stopped, it'd be over. Chrys shrieked in alarm as the oil-slick darkness drew closer. My lungs burned as I ran for safety, as I ran for Lucas. I didn't know how I knew it, but I knew if I could just make it to him, I'd be safe. I tripped, sliding on the rough gravel. I scrambled to my feet, but the darkness grabbed me, crushing me under it. I writhed and screamed, but I couldn't break free.

Chapter 23

Lucas

BY THE TIME WE GOT BACK TO MY PLACE, there was another car parked behind Nolan's. I hadn't expected him until tomorrow, but that wasn't a problem—I had some wild-caught salmon in the freezer I could pull out to thaw. Add in some fresh lemon and rosemary, pop it all on the grill, and he'd be happy.

"Looks like Sean made it. Wonder if he's asked Melanie out yet."

I snorted at Nolan's non sequitur. It had been obvious to the rest of us that Sean had been harboring an unrequited crush on Nolan's sister for years, but as far as we knew, Nolan was oblivious.

"How long have you known?"

He shrugged. "Just since I realized that he looks at Melanie the same way you look at Miriam." He pegged me with a look. "The question is, do I give him a hard time to push him to act, or do I hype him up, so he knows I support him?"

"Or you could just leave him alone and let him work it out himself."

"Nah. I kinda want to mess with him. That bear is fun to poke."

"I'm pretty sure there's a saying about how that's a bad idea."

Nolan looked thoughtful, then shook his head. "Not familiar with that one."

"It literally goes, 'Don't poke the bear.'"

He shook his head again. "Not ringing a bell. Come on, this will be fun. I've always wanted to play over-protective older brother."

I silently begged Sean for forgiveness for any part I unwittingly played in his future misery. Then, I followed Nolan inside, wondering just how bad this train wreck was going to be.

"I have a bone to pick with you," Nolan said the moment he saw Sean.

The bear shifter had been lounging on the couch, watching something on his phone, but at Nolan's proclamation, he looked up in confusion.

He glanced at me, and I shrugged and shook my head. "Ignore him. Can I get you anything to eat?"

"No," Nolan interjected, "he doesn't get food."

I smacked my friend upside his head. "You don't get to deny *my* guests food in *my* home."

"Ow!" Nolan exclaimed, rubbing the back of his head. "That actually hurt."

"Good! You should know better! You don't get to stomp all

over gnomish hospitality just because you want to play overprotective older brother."

Nolan grimaced. "Right, sorry."

"Do I want to know?" Sean asked.

Nolan stomped up to him. "I know about Melanie."

Sean paled. "I've gotta take this." He motioned to his darkened phone, then bolted off the couch and out the door.

"Huh. I've never seen a bear shifter move that fast." Nolan looked thoughtful for a minute, then grinned mischievously. "This is going to be so much fun."

I couldn't decide if I should come to Sean's rescue or let it play out. I debated with myself while I cleaned the grill. Ultimately, I decided that Nolan's meddling might just be the push Sean needed to either ask Melanie out or move on.

After cleaning the grill, I threw together a mid-afternoon snack for my guests. Dylan wasn't back yet, and Sean was still hiding, but Nolan happily helped himself. Then, I headed over to the conservatory to check on my students' projects.

I went around to the side of the main building, scanning my badge at the entrance to the classrooms. Then, down the hall, out another door, through the Butterfly Garden, and down a winding tree-lined gravel path, take the left fork, and arrive at the university greenhouse. I only made it a few steps into the building before beating a hasty and *silent* retreat—nobody wanted their professor to crash their date. I made a mental note to go back over the rules of use for the greenhouse on Monday while making subtle eye contact with the perpetrator.

I hurried back up the path and took the other fork. This path led to my favorite place in the conservatory. I rounded the bend and stepped out of the dappled shade cast by the trees. A clear spring greeted me, its quiet burbling filling the tranquil air. This spring was one of the best-kept secrets in the entire conservatory. Away from the main attractions, this small spring didn't garner much attention from tourists, and that was precisely part of its charm.

The air here felt more saturated with magic than normal. The springs in the conservatory held minor magical properties, which created various micro-climates and allowed certain flora to flourish here that would not have otherwise survived in this environment. I wasn't an Arizona native, but when I'd visited back when applying to colleges as a high school senior, I'd immediately felt drawn to this place. It was like a giant sign had lit up in my mind that said, 'You belong here,' and the thought of having to leave had made me physically ill.

The day I was accepted had been one of the best days of my life, and I couldn't wait to move out here. I begged my family to come visit. Something about this place was magnetic—wild dragons couldn't have pulled me away. I was so certain my family would feel the same way I did, but they didn't. They said the place was nice, but they couldn't feel the magic here like I could. After a few days, they left to go back home, and I stayed behind.

Sometimes Azalea and Dad still tried to get me to move back home and rejoin the family business, but I couldn't. They didn't understand the connection I felt, and I couldn't explain. I felt stronger here, more grounded. I could access my nature magic more easily than I had anywhere else. The plants responded readily, and I could affect changes in them that shouldn't have been possible, like my dwarf hibiscus. Even more, encouraging the plants to grow here took a fraction of the power it used to.

After years of living in cheap student apartments in Phoenix, I happened across the listing for my house. I'd been lucky to find a home so close to the conservatory and its magic water, close enough that I could still get a minor power boost in my own home.

Today, the magic was nearly suffocating. I drew it in with every inhale and released it as I exhaled. The feeling of magic flowing through me was heady, and I fought the temptation to hold onto it. Anyone with a lick of magic knew better than to hold onto any that wasn't their own. Only guardians could hold onto other magic without risking burning out, or worse.

***

There were still a few cars parked in front of The Booklight when I drove to pick Miriam up, so I had to park a few stores down. I didn't mind, though. The night was warm, and if I played my cards right, I'd get to hold her hand on the walk back. That thought alone nearly had me parking further away.

I'd just climbed out of my car when a scream rent the air.

"Let me go! HELP! LUCAS!"

Miriam's voice tore through me, and my heart froze in fear. Just outside the store, a man held Miriam captive and was dragging her away. Fury ripped through me when I saw who it was.

"Let her go!"

Jason's head snapped around as he looked at me over his shoulder, but he didn't stop. Instead, he threw Miriam over his shoulder. By the way she was convulsing, she had to be in the middle of a seizure.

"LUCAS!" she screamed again.

The sound of her terrified screams shredded my heart. I ran after Jason, yelling at my best friend to put my girlfriend down. I caught up to them just as he reached his SUV. I grabbed a fistful of his suit coat and pulled.

"Please, Jason, don't do this. Just put her down—she's having a seizure."

He shook his head, his expression closed off. "I can't. I'm sorry … for everything."

Before I could respond, pain blossomed across my face. My head snapped back, and my vision swam, growing darker as I sank to the ground. The last thing I saw was my former friend throwing my girlfriend into the backseat of his SUV.

Chapter 24

Lucas

CONSCIOUSNESS RETURNED WITH A SLEDGEHAMMER and an incessant ringing. I sat up and immediately regretted it. My surroundings wavered, and the horizon tilted as I once again found myself prone on the ground. Something in my pocket vibrated, and the ringing in my head spiked to even more painful levels. I pulled my phone out of my pocket to find the screen lighting up as it buzzed in my hand. I jabbed at the green button but missed. I tried again and got it.

"'Lo?" The single syllable was all I could manage.

The words that came out the other end were garbled and unintelligible. I shook my head, and pain lanced through it.

"No … taken … Miriam …" It took everything in me just to get those words out.

The only thought my brain could latch onto was that Miriam was gone. More garbled noise came from the phone, and I hung up. If they weren't going to help me find Miriam, there was no point continuing to talk to them.

***

I came to in a hospital room, the beeping of the machines a counterpoint to the throbbing in my head.

Miriam. I need to find Miriam. The need to find and protect her was nearly suffocating. My magic roiled within me, unsettled and vengeful.

I struggled to sit up, but firm hands pushed me back down.

"No. Miriam. He's got Miriam."

"Who's got Miriam?"

I struggled to focus enough to figure out who was talking. Three figures hovered at my bedside, and it took a minute for my vision to clear, though my left eye remained blurry.

"Who's got Miriam?" Dylan repeated.

"My girlfriend. He's got her. He's got Miriam." I was like a broken record, my mind stuck on a singular thought.

"Who. Has. Miriam?" Dylan enunciated each word. "Think carefully. What happened?"

"He took her. Went to pick her up, but he dragged her off while she was screaming … screaming my name. I tried … I tried to stop him, but he took her anyway."

Even in my befuddled state, I didn't miss the look that passed between my friends, equal parts pity and horror.

"He who?"

"Jason." I spat his name like a curse.

I struggled to sit up again, and once again, my friends

pushed me back down.

"Jason? Our Jason took Miriam, your girlfriend?" Dylan asked.

"Yes," I growled. *What part of that was hard to understand?*

"Why would he kidnap her?" Nolan asked.

I strained against my friends' hands, the *need* to get out and rescue Miriam burning in my veins and clearing out some of the fog in my head.

"I don't know, but I think it has to do with why I called the intervention. If I'd known he was talking about *Miriam*, I would have laid him out right then."

Bile burned in my throat when I thought about how he'd talked about her. He didn't love her and didn't plan on ever loving her, but he was going to force her to marry him. All because of some shifter politics I didn't understand. My fury swept the remaining cobwebs out of my mind, and I pushed my friends off me as I explained the conversation I'd had with Jason a few days ago.

I pulled off the various cords attached to me, and their corresponding monitors began shrieking.

"That makes no sense," Sean muttered. "Why would they target your girlfriend? I mean no offense, I'm sure she's a lovely person, but she doesn't seem important enough merit all this trouble."

I wanted to snap at him and say that Miriam was *the* most important person in the world, in *my* world, but he was right. *Why Miriam?* Then again, it didn't matter why, not to me. I was going to get her back, and nothing was going to stop me.

A nurse hurried into the room and moved to intercept me. "Sir," she said, "you're injured. You need to lie back down."

"No. I will sign whatever paperwork you need me to sign, but I'm leaving."

"I hear that you're eager to leave, but you were assaulted, and you just woke up. I need you to at least wait until the doctor checks on you."

"We'll make sure he stays," Dylan grunted.

I glared at him.

He shrugged. "You can't rescue your girl if you're half dead from your injuries. What did he do to you anyway?"

I winced. "He punched me." I felt like a wuss saying that. *Who gets knocked out and then hospitalized by a single punch to the face?*

Dylan grunted again. "He must have used his shifter strength to make sure you went down hard and fast."

That made me feel a little better. Griffins were strong, even for shifters.

"Well, that explains his face, but it doesn't explain Miriam," Sean pointed out.

"I … have a … theory …" Dylan said slowly, casting a worried glance in my direction.

"Out with it," I snapped.

"Sit first," he replied, pointing to the bed.

I huffed but sat. We all looked at Dylan expectantly and he shifted uncomfortably.

"I ... have reason to believe that your girlfriend is ... a seer."

I was glad I was sitting because my legs suddenly had no strength.

"She can't be a seer," I denied it automatically. She couldn't be, because if she was, the griffins would never let her go. Seers were the rarest type of supernatural, and therefore, valuable. No supernatural group would ever let a seer go once they had one in their clutches. She was just human. She had to be, because if she wasn't, I'd never get her back. "She can't be—she has seizures."

"Oh no," Nolan said, and all heads swiveled to look at him.

"What did you do?" I demanded.

He winced, his shoulders climbing up to his ears. "Please don't hate me."

"What did you do?"

"Remember how I said Jason needed my help for a case? Well ... he needed me to make a placebo for a type of seizure medication."

I froze as the pieces clicked into place. "The break-in. He switched out her seizure medication. The seizures were visions." I paused. "Humans don't get familiars. It's not some unknown supernatural ancestor." I looked around wildly. "Where's Chrys?"

"Gone," Dylan said. "I imagine Jason grabbed her after he finished with you."

I didn't know if I should be grateful that they had each other or furious that Jason likely had both of them. I rose to my feet, filled with determination. I was going to rescue Miriam, even if it killed me.

An hour, a disapproving doctor, and a stack of paperwork later and I was seated in Dylan's SUV while he drove us home. My face throbbed to the beat of my pulse. The doctor's words about possible skull fractures and my definite concussion swirled around my head. My left eye was still blurry, the area around it tender and swollen. I'd left before they could do any scans, so they weren't sure just how bad my injuries were. But I couldn't stay, not when Miriam was missing. The need to find her burned in my chest, spurring me on when my body demanded rest.

We drove past the conservatory, and something invisible yanked on my chest. I jerked up and gasped for breath as the pull continued to increase.

"Stop!" I gasped, and Dylan slammed on the breaks.

I fumbled with the door handle and tumbled out of the SUV before my friends could stop me. I struggled to my feet but found my way blocked by Dylan.

"Move," I gasped.

"No. You're going to go home and rest. You can barely stay on your feet. You are no good to Miriam like this. I put in a call to my team; they're en route to your house. When they get here, we'll come up with a plan. Until then, you're benched."

Chapter 25

Miriam

REALITY RETURNED, and I found myself sprawled out in the backseat of an unfamiliar SUV. Any hope I had that Lucas had picked me up and was taking me home was dashed when I saw the driver.

"You," I spat, even as my heart clenched in fear. All I received in response was a grunt.

This is bad. This is very bad. I didn't know what he wanted with me, but I knew I needed to get away.

I slowly sat up, hating to let him know that I was conscious again, but I couldn't escape while lying down. A soft chirp near my stomach drew my attention, and I found Chrys nestled next to me in her bowl. I scooped her up and cradled her against me, her concern whispering through my mind. I stroked her head with a finger, silently comforting her.

I looked out the window and squinted into the darkness. From what I could tell, we were still within the city limits. Unfortunately, we were going too fast for me to risk jumping. Even as I thought about attempting an escape that way, I realized I couldn't risk it, not with Chrys and her eggs. I could withstand a bit of jostling, but catapulting a couple of precious eggs out of a fast-moving vehicle was a bad idea.

It's fine. We'll figure it out. We'll take the first chance we get.

We drove in silence for a few more minutes while I tried to figure out where we were. The streetlights were growing farther and farther apart. In the distance, there was a stoplight at the crossroads. I stared at it, willing the colors to change.

Red. Red. Come on.

It flipped to yellow, and a second later, to red. We slowed to a stop, and I yanked on the door handle, jumping out before it was fully open. I hit the ground and took off running, Chrys' bowl in hand. I heard a door slam shut behind me, and I sprinted harder. There was a scuffling noise in the dirt behind me, and a strong arm grabbed me around the waist. A large hand wrapped around my throat and squeezed.

I woke up in the car with my hands cuffed together, and Chrys was gone. A glass partition was up between the front and back seats.

"Where is my familiar?" I demanded as I banged on the partition, wishing it would shatter and embed itself in his face.

My heart beat wildly, and my panic rose as my skin crawled.

"She's up here with me. She'll be fine. You just need to behave."

I couldn't see her from where I was, and the seatbelt latch wouldn't release, so I couldn't move around to try and catch a glimpse of her. I sat back, feeling defeated. My breath came in gasps, and my heart hurt like someone was squeezing it. My hands and feet tingled, the sensation crawling up my arms. I trembled and shook and shivered as tears tracked down my face. If things were bad before, they were even worse now.

This man was a SAID agent, and I looked like a criminal. Even if I managed to escape, between the handcuffs and his badge, it would take no effort for him to convince people that I was a criminal instead of a victim—they might even help him catch me. And he had Chrys. As long as he had her, he had my compliance, and he knew it. But that begged the question—what could he possibly want with me?

My thoughts spun around and around in an ever-worsening spiral of doom.

I don't know how long we drove, but I was exhausted when we got there. Agent Stone parked, then hauled me out of the car, a firm hand wrapped around my arm. We walked up to a darkened porch, and he unlocked the door, pushing me in ahead of him. I tripped on the lip and went sprawling.

"Get up," he growled impatiently.

I struggled to my feet, and he pushed me into a darkened room off to the side. A moment later, the light flicked on, and I blinked rapidly as my eyes adjusted. Next thing I knew, I was being forced back into a chair and tied to it.

"Why are you doing this?" I demanded, tears threatening again.

"Trying to keep you safe," he replied without looking at me.

"Safe!?" I choked on the word. "You think kidnapping me, knocking me unconscious, and tying me to a chair is keeping me *safe*? What is wrong with—" he shoved a gag in my mouth, cutting me off abruptly.

I howled in rage, the sound muffled by the fabric in my mouth.

"Be. Quiet. You have no idea what's going on right now."

No idea? I'm pretty sure kidnapping is what's going on.

As if reading my thoughts, he continued. "There are others out there that want you for nefarious reasons. I took you to keep you safe from them. It is my ... responsibility to keep you safe."

So, you stalked me and then kidnapped me ... to keep me safe? Wow, you are on the crazy train straight to Delulu Town. It's not like there were other *options available, like, I don't know, talking, maybe? Nope, that wasn't a viable option at all. Absolutely had to jump straight to kidnapping. And since when is it* your *responsibility to keep* me *safe? You don't even seem to want that responsibility—you can give it back.*

My inner voice was full of snark and sarcasm, but it was the only thing keeping me grounded, so I let it fly.

He stood. "Stay put and don't try anything—I still have your *griffin*," he sneered a little as he said the word. "I need to get a few supplies—I'll be back soon."

I hope she bites you. And what supplies do you need? Duct tape and a shovel?

My heart beat frantically at that thought, and I took a few deep breaths as I fought off another panic attack. Now was not the time to lose it. He left, turning the light off as he went. My fear ratcheted up several notches.

People know you're missing. Lucas *knows you're missing. He won't rest until you're found.*

I was more grateful for Lucas now than ever before. If this

had happened just last week, no one would have known I was gone for days.

You'll be found. You, Chrys, and the eggs will all make it out of here, and then you can spend an entire day cuddling with Lucas.

I clung to that slender thread of hope with all my might. I pictured us sitting on his couch, me curled against his side as we watched a lighthearted rom-com. I imagined us wandering his greenhouse, stealing kisses between the rows. But above all, I pictured the feeling of safety I always felt around him. Never again would I take feeling *safe* for granted.

Chapter 26

Lucas

I LAY ON MY BED, trying to ignore the visceral tug in my chest. It was like an invisible force had grabbed hold of me and was physically pulling me, and with every minute that I delayed, it got stronger.

Dylan's team still wasn't here, and every moment that ticked by had me imagining a new and worse fate for Miriam.

Soon, I couldn't take the pressure anymore and rolled to my feet. I swiped my badge off my dresser. Then, feeling like a rebellious teen, I rearranged my pillows to look like I was sleeping and snuck out the window. I leaned against the wall for a moment to let the world stop spinning.

I couldn't take my truck—I didn't have my keys, and I was in no shape to drive. I stumbled halfway down my driveway, then cut across the undeveloped land that separated my drive from the conservatory. This was technically part of the conservatory but remained untouched partly for a natural habitat for local wildlife and partly to provide a buffer between them and any neighbors.

Soon, I was stumbling across the parking lot. My normal

short commute was beginning to feel like a marathon. The conservatory was closed by this time of the night, so no one was here to see the spectacle or accidentally run me over. Eventually I made it to the door but had to lean against the wall while I struggled to scan my badge.

After the tenth try or so, I finally got it right and wrestled the door open. I practically fell into the building, only managing to catch myself at the last moment. I continued on, the tug in my chest pulling me deeper into the conservatory.

I found myself retracing my steps from earlier today. Down the hall, out a side door, down a gravel path, down the right-hand path. I collapsed by the spring, the air thick with magic. It pressed against my skin, almost tangible in its demand to be let in, and I didn't have the strength to refuse it.

I opened myself up to the flow of magic, but when I tried to direct it out of me, it sank deeper, suffusing my cells with its energy. The throbbing in my face and head lessened, and I closed my eyes as relief washed over me.

I need to find Miriam. The thought burned in my soul, but for the moment, I couldn't move. Magic continued to flow into me, and I desperately sought a way to siphon some of it off. Turning my senses to the soft grass under me, I channeled the magic down and out, the energy burning slightly as it passed through me. I was surprised when information began returning. There was a colony of ants five feet away, a rabbit's burrow seven feet in the other direction, and countless insects in the grass. The roots had formed a living network of communication.

Find Miriam. I sent the instructions out with the magic, holding a picture of her in my mind. I didn't know if it would work, but I had to try. I sent the magic out in an ever-growing circle, sweeping through the conservatory with hardly a thought. Then I hit the parking lot, and my progress came to a screeching halt. I raged against the lack of nature as I sought ways around these blind spots.

The magic poured through me in an uncontrollable torrent, and I felt my strength and resolve weakening. *How could I expect this to work?* We lived in a desert. Between the arid environment and mankind's infrastructure, there would be large swaths of land invisible to me. I didn't even know what my range was with this, but Miriam was probably beyond it anyway. The amount of information that came back to me was staggering. I couldn't process any of it—it was too much. My mind felt like it was going to collapse under the assault.

I was on the verge of giving up when a tiny weight settled on my chest, vibrating slightly. It moved up, tucking itself under my chin, grounding me. The deluge of magic slowed to a trickle, and I became aware of a pinprick of energy to the east, drawing me in like a homing beacon. I sent the magic out, focusing on reaching that speck of energy.

On and on, the magic crawled, from the wildflowers and grasses, to the trees, to the cacti and brush. It was easier outside the city, as there were fewer roads to contend with, but still, it wasn't as fast as I wanted. I continued on, stretching, reaching for the speck of energy that drew me in like a magnet. I reached a massive sycamore tree with a vast network of roots that ran under the majority of a small settlement nearby. The tree led me to a small, rundown house.

The paint was peeling, and the yard overgrown. I circled the house, but the doors were shut, the windows closed, and the blinds drawn. I couldn't see inside, but I knew without a shadow of a doubt that what I sought was within.

I reached for the weeds growing in a crack in the porch and sent them extra energy. Under my command, they grew and stretched, sending tendrils under the door. *There!* My blood boiled at what I saw, and I mentally screamed in rage. My connection to the plants severed under my anger and snapped my consciousness back into my body, the magic rebounding within me, making me feel like I was going to vibrate apart.

My stomach clenched, and I rolled over, heaving onto the ground. I shook as it felt like I was being torn apart by the magic. Something soft pressed into my throat, and the rebounding magic calmed until it formed a pool of power within me. I tried to let it drain out like I used to, but it refused to leave without direction. I pushed aside my worry—it was a problem for another time.

I rolled over onto my back and took several deep breaths before I dared to open my eyes. The sky was the dusty blue of pre-dawn, where the world drops its shroud of darkness just before the sun rises over the mountains. I'd been out here for hours.

A soft chirping drew my attention down to my chest, where a tiny cobalt blue teacup griffin perched, staring at me with obsidian eyes. His blue-black tail twitched as he took my measure.

A teacup griffin, just like Chrys. Is it possible?

"Hey there," I greeted him quietly. "Were you helping me with that magic?"

He chirped, and I felt the tiniest thrum of affirmation

whisper in my mind. I gasped, my heart clenching. "Are you my familiar?"

He chirped in affirmation again. Tears pricked the corners of my eyes. I never thought I'd be lucky enough to have a familiar of my own. I wanted to leap for joy, but the pressing *need* to find Miriam swamped me with guilt for my personal excitement. I could celebrate later—right now, I needed to get Miriam back. The image of her bound and gagged, with tear stains on her cheeks, sent a wave of white-hot fury coursing through me. The pool of power within me churned, begging to be unleashed. My familiar chirped, calming the raging in my blood, just as he had done earlier.

"Thank you," I said as I gently stroked his head with a finger. "I would have burnt up if it weren't for you."

I tried to sit up, but my limbs were jelly and refused to cooperate. The phone in my pocket buzzed, and with great effort, I managed to free it and jab the green button, but it slipped out of my fingers as I raised it. The phone smacked me in the face as it fell and landed next to my head.

"Where are you?" Dylan barked from the other end. "We've been trying to reach you for hours."

I grimaced. I hadn't intended to be gone for so long. My friends must have been worried sick after finding I was missing. Though, to be fair, they wouldn't have let me leave, and if I hadn't left, I wouldn't have found Miriam.

"...could have been dead in a ditch somewhere. What were you thinking?" I tuned back in to find that Nolan now had the phone. "Do you have any idea how worried we were? I thought you were dead." He sniffed. "Don't scare us like that."

"Where are you? We'll come get you." It was Dylan this time—he must have taken the phone back from Nolan.

"At the conservatory."

There was a long pause. "What do you remember from last night?"

"Do you mean the part where my *ex*-friend kidnapped my girlfriend, or the part where he hit me so hard I woke up in the hospital?" I snapped, my temper flaring.

"So, you remember Miriam was taken, and you still went to work?" The disapproval in his voice was almost a tangible thing. "I should make you walk home."

"It's not like that," I snapped again. "I *needed* to come here. And I'm glad I did. I found her, Dyl. I found Miriam." I proceeded to give a garbled explanation of what happened and was greeted with a long bout of silence on the other end.

"Can you get to the parking lot?" he asked after a long moment.

"No," I replied. "I can't move at all." The words tasted bitter in my mouth. I'd found Miriam, but I was too weak to do anything about it.

"Then don't. I'm on my way."

"Wait. You need a badge."

"You're outside, right?"

"Yeah."

"Then, no. I don't."

He must have passed the phone over to Nolan because the woodland fae jabbered in my ear about something, but I was too tired to concentrate. The sound of leathery wings filled the air as dirt swirled around me. The last thing I saw before sleep claimed me was a majestic red dragon touching down beside my spring.

Tesha Geddes

Chapter 27

Lucas

I WOKE UP TO FIND MYSELF SPRAWLED OUT on my couch, surrounded by my friends.

"Rise and shine sleeping beauty," Dylan grunted. "What were you saying about finding Miriam?"

"Dylan," Nolan chided, "he just woke up. Give him a minute to recover before you start grilling him."

"She might not *have* a minute," Dylan grumbled. "Our raid turned up no trace of her. Wherever Jason took her, it's not on our radar."

"Wait, hold up. What raid?" I asked, feeling lost.

"I reported Miriam's kidnapping, as well as your statement about Jason. It was enough to get a warrant to raid the griffin clan house as well as any of Jason's personal property. He lived at the clan house though, so that was a moot point. Regardless, neither of them was there, and his father denies any knowledge of a potential seer. Jason's gone to ground, and we can't find him. So, what did you find out? And how?"

I took a deep breath and closed my eyes as I tried to recall

all the details. "He took her to a house somewhere east of here. I don't know the exact address; but if I saw it again, I'd recognize it."

"And how did you come across this information?"

I looked down guiltily. "I channeled the magic of the spring to search for her. The plants found her for me."

"You channeled outside magic?!" That was Sean—his stricken face made me grimace. "Do you have any idea how dangerous that was? You could have died!"

"Hmm, possibly," Dylan said.

"What do you mean 'hmm, possibly?'" Sean demanded. "Everyone knows that channeling magic like that is a great way to burn out and die."

"Except for guardians," Dylan pointed out.

"Do you see any guardians here?" Sean snapped. "He could have died! And you're being so blasé about it."

I grimaced. I'd never seen Sean like this before—I must have really freaked him out.

Dylan simply raised an eyebrow, then looked at me. "Hey, Lucas. How's your face feeling?"

My brows furrowed. "Fine … why?"

He shrugged. "You're looking pretty good for someone who had a massive knuckle sandwich last night."

Nolan leaned over and poked my face near my left eye. "You're right! Wasn't this swollen shut last night?"

I reached up to feel the area myself. It felt fine, and my headache was gone. "How …?"

Dylan sat back and crossed his arms. "How much do you know about guardians and seers?"

I sat up, curious. "Not much, just that guardians protect places and can channel magic, and seers are humans that have visions."

Dylan nodded. "Guardians typically protect lands where a lot of magic has pooled, reservoirs of magic, if you will. Some positions are hereditary, others are chosen, with the choosing being done by the magical land in question."

I nodded—all of this sounded familiar.

"Then there's a much rarer type of guardian that is called to protect both a land *and* a person. This type of guardianship is always chosen, never inherited, and the land, while steeped in magic, is not nearly on the same scale as other reservoirs of magic."

"And the people they're supposed to protect?" I prompted when he paused.

"Almost always a seer."

"You think I'm Miriam's guardian?"

Dylan nodded, and my mind whirled. Was this why I was so sensitive to the magic in the springs? Could a nerdy half-elf, half-gnome really be a guardian? And, if I *was* chosen to protect Miriam, did that mean my feelings were all a by-product of this magic? My heart clenched at the thought. *Magic can't manufacture love, right? That's still a rule ... isn't it? I guess that begs the question, is what I feel for Miriam love, or is it derived from possibly being her guardian?* I thought about her warm brown eyes and how attentively she listened every time I rambled on about one of my experiments or my plants. I thought about how the sound of her laughter warmed my soul and how her head fit perfectly in the hollow beneath my shoulder. I thought about how much I wanted to pull her into my arms and kiss her until she was breathless and then kiss her some more. Every time I pictured my future, she was by my side. If this wasn't love yet, it was well on its way. No magic needed.

"What now?" I asked. "How do I use this," I waved my hand around vaguely, "to save her?"

There was a soft fluttering sound, and a tiny weight landed on my head. I reached up to pet my familiar, a feeling of determination flowing through our bond.

"I should have known he'd bond with you," Dylan said with a chuckle. At my look of confusion, he continued, "I believe that is Chrys' mate. If you're the seer's guardian, it makes sense that you'd bond with her familiar's mate."

I paused as a thought occurred to me. "How did he get here?"

"Remember how I said I had a lead up here on my latest case?"

I nodded.

"The lead was Miriam and Chrys—she had a premonition that led me right to the people keeping him illegally." He scowled. "I walked in on Jason hitting on her … unsuccessfully. She kept turning him down, even said she had a boyfriend, but he wouldn't take 'no' for an answer. Now I know why. I ended up having to escort him out of there."

I stood as rage thundered through me. Power coursed through my veins, and I saw red. I couldn't fault him for flirting at first, but the fact that he didn't accept the rejection made me livid. *Was he the creep Miriam told me about?* If he didn't listen to her say no, then what *else* might he not listen to? The need to rescue her rose in me like a tangible thing. It swirled within me, fueled by my anger. Rising. Rising. Rising.

"Lucas! Snap out of it!"

I became aware of Dylan shaking me, shouting my name. I looked around. My living room was a wreck. Thick, thorny vines had burst from the ground, shattering the tile and strangling the furniture and my friends. Dylan had cut himself free with his talons. Sean had completely shifted, but even his bear claws weren't enough to get through the vines. I released the magic holding the vines in place, and they shriveled and died.

"I'm sorry—I didn't mean … I'm sorry," I stammered out an apology, horrified that I'd hurt my friend because I couldn't control my temper and my new magic.

I sank back onto the couch as the rage left, feeling depleted.

"So … nobody else flirt with Miriam—Lucas does not handle jealousy well," Nolan joked, his laugh sounding forced.

Dylan and Sean glared at him.

"I'm not jealous," I protested.

"Suuure you're not," Nolan said. "That's why you destroyed your living room when you heard someone else was flirting with your girl."

"I'm not. I'm angry and … afraid. I'm angry that he didn't listen the first time she told him 'no,' and I'm afraid of what other 'no's' he might ignore. I … I don't want to think it of him, but he already kidnapped her—clearly, he's not too concerned about consent."

My words landed heavily, and a suffocating silence descended on the room. Judging by their faces and lack of eye contact, none of my friends wanted to think that of Jason either, but it was hard to argue with his recent actions. A large part of me wanted there to be a logical, reasonable explanation, but I also couldn't sit back and trust that all would be well. Miriam was mine to protect, whether I was her guardian or not, and I wouldn't rest until I was certain she was safe.

"Dylan, do you still have access to that drone?"

He nodded.

"Get it. We're finding Miriam."

Chapter 28

Miriam

True to his word, Agent Stone wasn't gone long. But what supplies he needed remained a mystery. He brought Chrys in with him and set her on the coffee table in the center of the room.

My stomach growled, reminding me that I hadn't eaten. I sensed Chrys' echoing hunger pangs and an ache that had settled in her bones. I tried to get the agent's attention to let him know that we needed to eat and that Chrys needed her medicine, but he steadfastly ignored all my attempts at communication. I added that to his growing list of sins and character defects.

My stomach growled again, and I thought hungrily of Lucas' cooking. I'd been looking forward to dinner all day. I had no idea what was planned, but if Lucas was cooking, it was sure to be good. I glared at Agent Stone for making me miss it. Maybe Lucas would save me some. Who was I kidding? When I got back, Lucas would make me a banquet of all my favorite foods. When, not if, because Chrys and I *were* going to escape. We would make it back to Lucas, no matter what it took.

After walking the house twice to make sure it was secure,

the agent stretched himself out on the couch and promptly fell asleep. I seethed internally. *How dare he make himself comfortable while I'm tied to a chair like some kind of criminal. Keeping me safe, my foot! If he was really concerned about my safety, he'd get me something to eat and let me lie down.*

I dozed off and on all night in the uncomfortable chair. My only consolation was that Agent Stone didn't seem to sleep that well either—he got up every hour to walk the perimeter of the house and check the windows.

I was running down a gravel path, the stones crunching under my feet. Chrys shrieked, her panic spiraling through me, urging me on. Darkness encroached behind me, almost solid in its presence. Out on the path ahead of me, an unwelcome figure appeared. I mentally cursed but kept going. Better the devil you know than the devil you don't. If I could just make it around him, I knew Lucas would be right there, and if I could make it to Lucas, I'd be safe. Agent Stone raised his gun, aiming it at me. No. Not at me, at whatever chased me.

"*Go! Get to Lucas!*" *he shouted.*

Bang! Bang! Bang!

He fired shots off at the darkness, and I sped by, not waiting around to see if he hit anything.

Ahead of me, a figure stood on the path, wreathed in a golden glow. Though I couldn't see them clearly, I knew exactly who it was. I sobbed in relief. Lucas found me. All would be well.

I blinked and raised my head to look around. The pitch darkness of the room had lightened to gray, and dawn was not far off. The feeling of relief from my dream lingered until I remembered another detail. I mentally scowled. Agent Stone did *not* get to be the good guy here, and I was mad at my subconscious for trying to give him a redemption arc.

There will be no Stockholm Syndrome here. Not. Happening.

I tried to regain the sense of peace and hope the end of the dream had given me, but much like the night, it was rapidly fading. All that was left was the fear and awful certainty that *something* terrible was coming. Something *more* terrible, I mentally amended as I glanced at Agent Stone, who was methodically cleaning his gun.

He holstered his gun and checked the windows one more time.

"Time to go," he said.

I balked at the thought of going anywhere else. The more we moved, the less likely I would be found soon. Then again, the more we moved, the more chances I had at escaping.

He unbound me and hauled me to my feet but left my hands cuffed together. As I stood, I became aware of a very pressing need.

"Can I at least use the bathroom first?"

I thought he would refuse, but in the end, he pushed me down the hall and into a tiny bathroom and closed the door behind me.

"Two minutes."

Part of me wanted to push it, see how long I could stall, just to be contrary. But the larger, more sensible part of me did not want to be caught with my pants down ... literally. Going to the bathroom while handcuffed was not easy, but I somehow managed within my allotted time frame.

Unfortunately, even if I'd been uncuffed, the bathroom did not offer a viable escape route. Its only other exit was a small window that even my slight frame would have had a hard time fitting through.

All too soon, we were back on the road, with Chrys in the front, confined to a birdcage strapped to the seat. She chirped and shrieked angrily at being locked up. I mentally vowed that if we escaped ... *when* we escaped, no one would ever lock her in a cage again. Like last night, I was cuffed in the back seat, but this time, the partition was down.

My stomach had stopped growling, but I was starting to feel faint. My half-gnome boyfriend had spoiled me—just a couple days of three square meals, and my body had forgotten how to deal with being hungry.

"Do you ever plan on feeding me? Or do you intend on starving me to death and dumping my body in the desert?"

Agent Stone rummaged in a bag near him and something in a shiny wrapper landed on my lap.

"Quit being dramatic," he said.

"'Quit being dramatic,' says the guy who kidnapped me, handcuffed me, dragged me to the middle of nowhere, then tied me to a chair *all night*, and *caged* my familiar, refused to let me give her her medicine, never mind the fact that I haven't eaten since lunch yesterday. Oh, no, I have absolutely *no* reason to think my life might be in danger," I snarked quietly as I struggled with the wrapper. I was tired and hangry, and that made my lips looser than they should have been.

I finally managed to open the shiny package and took a bite. I wrinkled my nose, not bothering to hide my disgust. It was one of those stale protein bars that tasted like sawdust. I managed to choke it down while wishing I could use it to choke my captor. Death by health food—I could appreciate the irony.

I looked out the window, but aside from the road, we'd left all traces of civilization behind. All I could see were desert shrubs, scrubby juniper trees, and the occasional saguaro. Seeing the juniper trees reminded me of Lucas and our date tonight. Juniper berry tea. It might sound like a lame date to most people, but I'd been looking forward to it, especially if it involved any amount of kissing.

Chapter 29

Lucas

TRYING TO TRANSLATE WHAT I LEARNED from the plants to what the drone showed proved to be more difficult than I'd anticipated. Dylan was more patient with me than I was with myself.

"Try to pinpoint any major roads you crossed and narrow it down from there," he suggested.

The doorbell rang, and Dylan answered it while I struggled to figure out if I'd crossed this road or that.

"Got a lead on the seer yet?" a troll roughly the size of a fridge asked as he walked into my house with two others. One looked like a lean human man, but the way he carried himself with coiled energy convinced me he was a supernatural, likely a shifter. The last was a female elf.

"Potential seer," the man behind the troll corrected.

"Semantics," the troll grunted.

"It doesn't much matter if she is or isn't right now. Her kidnapper believes she is, and *that* is what's important," the elf said. "It may be the only thing keeping her alive."

From the looks of it, this was Dylan's SAID team. While I was grateful for their help, their presence made this all the more horrifyingly real. His team continued to converse in hushed tones while I turned my whole focus to finding Miriam. As their host, I should have been offering them refreshments, but that didn't matter right now. Nothing mattered except Miriam.

"What happened over there?" the lean man asked as he pointed to my living room, sounding horrified.

"Long story," Dylan grunted. "Pull up a chair. This is Lucas—he has a lead on where the seer's being kept. Once we get an address, we'll file for a warrant and be on our way."

If there was more conversation after that, I tuned it out.

I directed the drone farther and farther to the east. I passed a massive sycamore tree, and my heart leapt. It was the same tree, I was sure of it. I slowed down and studied the houses individually. Many of the buildings were just as rundown as the one I'd seen, but I soon found it.

"That one, right there," I said, pointing to the screen.

Dylan took over the screen and pulled up the coordinates and, from there, the address.

"Everyone, load up. A judge will work on the warrant while we drive," he said, and his team sprang into action.

I followed them out the door, my familiar buzzing around my shoulders.

"No civilians," the lean man said, stopping me as I was about to climb into the van with him.

I glared at him. I was going to save Miriam, and he was in the way. My familiar landed on my shoulder, and I felt my connection to the land open up. A vine shot out of the ground and wrapped around the agent before lifting him up and bodily throwing him away. He landed on his feet with a surprising amount of grace and agility—I'd stake my *Vanilla planifolia* on him being some sort of cat shifter. The troll looked at me warily while the elf regarded me with disdain.

Dylan simply shrugged and told me to get my rear in the van instead of holding them up. I climbed in and claimed a seat, immediately feeling out of place. The van looked like a mobile armory, and I was cautious not to touch anything. My familiar perched on my shoulder and began preening.

Dylan passed the keys to the agent I'd thrown and climbed in next to me, his large frame barely managing to squeeze into the seat. The other agent took the keys and, with a wary glance at me, climbed into the driver's seat. Soon, we were all loaded up and pulling out of my drive. With two rows of two and one in the back, plus all the weapons, it was cramped.

"What's the deal with the half-elf?" the woman asked, her tone barely shy of a sneer.

I didn't give it any attention. By the looks of it, she was a full-blooded elf and had all the prejudices and airs that so frequently went with that.

"He has been and will continue to be instrumental in recovering the seer," Dylan answered, choosing his words with care.

The shifter in the driver's seat swore quietly. "He's the guardian, isn't he?"

The elf eyed me, looking at me like I was off-smelling meat. "Some guardian—he let the seer get kidnapped."

She was right. If I really was the guardian, I'd failed at my one job—to keep Miriam safe.

Dylan let out a low growl, and she flinched and turned her attention out the window.

"So, what'd you name him?" my friend asked, nodding to my familiar.

My stomach swooped as I was swamped with guilt. I was as terrible a keeper as I was a guardian. The teacup griffin had stunning deep blue feathers and blue-gray fur. Compared to Chrys' fluff, he was practically sleek. Where Chrys' feline half put me in mind of a ragdoll cat, he resembled a Russian Blue. *But what should I name him?* I looked down at him as if he would give me a clue. He simply regarded me with his intelligent black eyes.

I looked out the window for inspiration when a flash of blue in someone's lawn caught my eye. I had those same flowers in my front garden beds.

"Canterbury," I said decisively. I looked down at my familiar. "Does that work for you?" The teacup griffin chirped his approval.

Dylan looked at me with raised brows. "That's a big name for such a little guy."

The elf snorted.

"Agent Briarthorn, do we have a problem?" Dylan rumbled.

Even though it wasn't directed at me, I still shrank at the tone of his voice. The elf flinched but didn't back down.

"A guardian's familiar is supposed to help them protect the seer. How is such a *tiny* thing going to be of any use? How can someone with *half* the power of a full elf ever hope to be a guardian—he already let the seer get kidnapped. Are you sure *you* aren't the guardian?"

"Did you miss the part where he bodily threw me across the yard *with a vine*? Even *you* can't do that, Miss My-Bloodline's-Purer-Than-Yours-So-I'm-Better-Than-You," the shifter in the driver's seat snapped at her.

The troll grunted in agreement.

"Sorry for being concerned about the seer's safety—I just think she deserves a better guardian. Who lets their charge get taken so easily?"

She wasn't wrong—Miriam did deserve better. But, guardian or not, Miriam was my girlfriend, and I would do everything in my power to get her back and keep her safe.

"I seem to recall a young agent botching a simple recon mission and letting a criminal slip through their fingers their first week on the job," Dylan said quietly.

Somehow, his quiet voice was scarier than his growling one.

"That's different," she muttered mutinously.

"You're right, it is," Dylan agreed. "You had training and knew what you were supposed to do. He had neither training nor knowledge. You disobeyed orders and caused a two-week manhunt. He was a college professor who witnessed his girlfriend get kidnapped and ended up hospitalized when he tried to intervene. He didn't know he was a guardian or that she was a seer until after that."

By this point, Agent Briarthorn had sunk down in her seat, thoroughly chastised and embarrassed.

When you put it like that. It was nice to know that Dylan, at least, didn't consider me a failure. *If only I'd had this power when she was being taken.* I wanted to kick myself—I *could* have had this power if I'd opened myself to it and held onto it. Instead, I'd ignored every sign that my connection to the springs was different, that my growing powers were a sign of something more.

Canterbury chirped and rubbed his head against my neck, sending me a wave of reassurance. I gently stroked him as I struggled to pull myself out of my self-deprecating spiral. Miriam needed me to focus on rescuing her, not on my failures.

Chapter 30

Lucas

WE STOPPED AROUND THE CORNER FROM THE HOUSE. The entire SAID team piled out of the car and strapped on bullet-proof vests. Dylan passed a spare one to me and told me to stay behind him. By the time I'd managed to strap it on, everyone else had their weapons out, ready to go.

Dylan sent Agent Briarthorn and the troll (who I'd learned was simply called 'Brick') around to the back of the house. Dylan and the cat shifter, Agent Brown, led the way up to the front door.

I looked around, feeling like something was very, very wrong. The driveway was empty, and nothing stirred. There were no obvious signs of traps, but the feeling of wrongness persisted.

The driveway is empty ...

"Dylan," I hissed, "his car is gone."

The dragon shifter glanced over at the driveway, and though he said nothing, his jaw clenched.

I reached out with my magic. This far from my base of power, my connection to the land was sluggish and weak. Still, it was enough to tell me what I needed to know. That bright spot that had drawn me in earlier was gone.

"She's not here," I said as I stripped the vest off and stalked away.

Dylan glared at me, but he and Agent Brown continued anyway. They had to do their job and clear the house, but all that mattered to me was that Miriam wasn't there. I didn't want to see the place where she'd been, not if she wasn't there for me to hold.

I threw the vest down and sprawled on the grass, Canterbury on my chest. I closed my eyes and reached out with my magic, deepening my connection to the land. Despite the weak connection, I could feel her. I could feel her, but I couldn't follow her. I couldn't tell how far away she was, only what direction.

"Giving up already?" Agent Briarthorn sneered. "Some guardian."

"Agent Briarthorn, if you cannot keep yourself in check, you will be on desk duty *for a month,*" Dylan snapped.

Desk duty didn't sound too bad to me, but must have to the elf because she shut up.

"She's that way," I said, pointing southeast. "That's all I can tell you."

There was a soft grunt, then Brick asked, "How do you know?"

I opened my eyes and sat up. "I asked the plants."

"*You* can nature-speak?" Agent Briarthorn said, her complexion darkening as her face twisted.

It took me a moment to identify the emotion—jealousy. All elves (and half-elves) had a connection to plants. We could communicate with them on the most basic level: encouraging growth, identifying diseases, making them drop fruit or even limbs, repairing minor damage, etc. But to ask them a question unrelated to their immediate needs and have them answer was a rare ability.

Any other time, I might have gloated a little, but not now, not when Miriam was still in danger. Instead, I simply nodded and headed back to the van, the SAID team following on my heels. They'd managed to clear the house quickly and found no signs of where Jason and Miriam had gone next.

Did he know we were coming, or had this only ever been a pit stop?

Dylan stopped me as I was about to climb into the car and shoved the bulletproof vest back into my arms.

"You three head out on the highway. The guardian and I will try a different tactic."

If it had been anyone else, I would have protested and argued that I deserved to be in the van too. But it was Dylan—I trusted him and knew him well enough to know that he wasn't benching me.

We watched the van pull away, and when it was out of sight, I turned to my friend and asked, "What now?"

He gave me a toothy grin, looking almost feral. "Now, we fly."

Next thing I knew, I was being borne aloft in the talons of a giant red dragon. I gave a shout and grabbed onto whatever part of him I could reach. Canterbury shrieked and wormed his way into the dubious safety of my shirt.

"Warn me next time!" I yelled, the wind whipping my words away.

Dylan angled himself east, and we shot forward, the land speeding under us in a blur of browns, reds, and greens. I squeezed my eyes shut—elvish gnomes were not made for dragon flight.

After a time, Dylan slowed, then landed near a stand of junipers. He set me down and rumbled at me. I didn't speak dragon, but his meaning was clear. *Find Miriam.*

I dropped the vest and sank to the ground, one hand on a sagebrush, the other on the packed soil. I reached for my connection to the land while Canterbury flew out of my shirt and loudly scolded Dylan.

"I could use your help," I said to my familiar, cutting him off mid-tirade.

He dutifully landed on my head and strengthened my connection. It was weaker than I would have liked, but I was able to find Miriam, still to the southeast. I pointed out the direction, and Dylan scooped me up again.

We continued on like that, flying a distance, then landing to check Miriam's location like she was our northern star. I don't know how long we kept it up, but it felt like forever until I felt something new.

"She's close! Less than a mile away," I said.

Her presence blazed in my mind. Dylan nodded, then shifted back to his bipedal form, his clothing swathing him. Ordinarily, shifters couldn't shift with their clothing, but the government provided all shifter agents with magic bracelets that held their clothing during a shift.

"We'll go on foot from here," he said, then nodded at the vest in my hands. "Put that on."

I did so, even though I itched at the delay. We were so close. I led the way as we walked.

Chapter 31

Miriam

WE DROVE ON THE HIGHWAY for a while before turning off onto a dirt road that was little more than an opening in the sparse vegetation. I idly wondered if Lucas knew the names of all these plants. My heart clenched at the thought of him. Knowing Lucas, he would have reported me missing by now. *But are the police even looking for me? If they are, how will they ever find me?*

We were surrounded by miles and miles of empty desert. Agent Stone could dispose of me anywhere here, and I wouldn't be found for years. I shuddered at the thought of my body being left to rot in a shallow grave. My heart pounded wildly, and I struggled to steady my breathing.

In the front seat, Chrys shrieked loudly, and a pressure grew behind my eyes. I closed them, and a different scene unfolded in my mind.

I sat in the passenger seat of a large, silver pickup, the delicious aroma of Lucas' cooking wafting from the back seat. A brightly-colored flock of teacup griffins flitted around the back, two of them making a valiant attempt to break into the picnic basket.

"Where are we going?" I asked with a laugh.

Lucas grinned at me from the driver's seat. "I told you—it's a surprise."

I pouted and batted my eyes, but he didn't relent.

He reached out and threaded his fingers through mine, giving my hand a gentle squeeze. "Don't worry. We're almost there."

But I wasn't worried. Not with him—never with him. His thumb rubbed the back of my hand, sending shivers down my spine. Even after a few years together, I still felt like a twitterpated schoolgirl. I hoped wherever we were going was secluded.

As if sensing my thoughts, he gave me a lopsided grin, a twinkle in his eyes.

Soon, he pulled to a stop and parked the truck. I waited while he got out and came around to open my door.

"My lady," he said with an extravagant bow.

I snickered as I took his hand and climbed out. "My lord," I replied with my best wobbly curtsy.

He grinned and kissed my cheek before opening the back door, releasing the rowdy flock of teacup griffins. He grabbed the picnic basket while I grabbed the blanket.

I followed him down a narrow, twisting trail that led us into a small ravine. He led us to a stand of desert willows, their pink and white blossoms a beautiful splash of color against the arid landscape. We wove our way between the trees, the teacup griffins abandoning us in favor of the trumpet-like flowers.

The trees opened up to reveal a small spring merrily burbling away, a small stream leading out the other side. Minuscule fish darted to and fro in the crystal-clear water. Though this spring lacked the magic of those in Wellspring, it still had a magic all its own.

"It's beautiful," I breathed, turning to take in the entire view. "How did you find this place?"

He winked at me. "I have my ways."

I laughed, and we spread out the blanket in the shade of a tree. Once we were seated, I wasted no time digging into the delicious food that had been tantalizing me the entire drive.

"Sorry," I said at Lucas' look. "I'm hungry."

He gave me another lopsided grin and leaned forward to kiss me. "Never apologize to a gnome for enjoying their food."

I smiled and abandoned my plate in favor of kissing Lucas, one of my favorite pastimes. I had just wrapped my arms around his neck and pulled him closer when a gust of wind washed over us, bringing with it the sound of large feathery wings.

I scowled at the griffin standing a few feet away, a woman on his back. The woman hopped off, and the griffin shifted back into a most unwelcome sight.

I glared at Agent Stone, offended that he had somehow managed to worm his way into my daydreams. He was as unwelcome there as he was here.

We pulled into a narrow ravine, and he parked the car.

"Stay here," he grunted.

It wasn't like I had much of a choice. He had the partition up and the child locks engaged ... or whatever they were called in a government vehicle. He climbed out of the car and circled around to grab Chrys. My heart pounded in fear. Was he going to leave her here? Was he going to abandon her in the middle of the desert and drive off without her? She had eggs to protect! She wouldn't be able to get food for herself, and with her injuries, she wouldn't be able to fly to safety. For the thousandth time, I cursed myself for not checking the door before I answered it. If I'd been just a little more careful, Agent Stone never would have gotten me.

My spiral of doom was interrupted by my door opening and the aforementioned evil agent hauling me out of the vehicle. He dragged me down the ravine and then ducked into a cave to the left.

As far as caves went, there was nothing special about this one. It was dry and dusty but cool. It was maybe ten feet deep and just high enough that Agent Stone didn't have to duck. At least it was spring and not summer. An enforced camping trip with no gear when the temperature could climb to over 110°F would be downright deadly.

Agent Stone forced me to sit at the back of the cave, tucked in a corner, out of sight. My heart beat wildly, the force of its pounding almost painful. I struggled to breathe, feeling like a dragon was sitting on my chest. My stomach twisted itself into knots, and I was suddenly grateful it was empty. The SAID agent crouched next to me and put his hand on my back. I flinched from his touch, and he removed his hand.

"Put your head between your knees and breathe," he instructed.

I glared at him. The last thing I wanted was my kidnapper coaching me through an anxiety attack.

Five things I can see ... Chrys, cave walls, dirt, my shoes ... and that lizard over there. The tiny critter skittered out of sight the moment I noticed him. *Four things I can hear ... my breathing, Chrys chirping, the wind, my kidnapper breathing down my neck. Okay, that last one wasn't helpful. Three things I can touch ... my shirt, the dirt, my pants. Two things I can smell ...* I inhaled deeply. *Ugh! Myself ... and Agent Stone doesn't smell like a rose either. One thing I can taste ... that I need to brush my teeth.*

The exercise might have reminded me of how gross I felt, but it had calmed me.

"That's it," Agent Stone said, patting me on the back, "just keep breathing."

I shuddered, my shoulders rising to my ears. He pulled his hand back and was silent for a moment.

"I know you have no reason to believe me, but I really am just trying to keep you safe."

I couldn't look at him. "You're right—I don't believe you."

Chrys shrieked, and pressure built up behind my eyes. I rubbed them with my shackled hands, and the world around me dissolved.

I was running down a gravel path. Behind me, griffins fought. One stood against four, another two lay bleeding on the ground. The four griffins were trying to get to me, but the fifth stopped them at every turn. He fought valiantly, but even he couldn't hope to keep on like this. I sprinted down the path, knowing one thing for certain—I needed Lucas.

Reality returned, and the agent's stony expression greeted me. His was definitely not the face I wanted to see after a seizure. In fact, if I never woke up to his face again, I would consider it a blessing.

"What did you see?" he demanded.

"What?"

"What. Did. You. See?" he repeated.

"You … want to know what I hallucinated about?" Was I understanding him correctly? Was he really going to try and play therapist right now?

He sat back with a sigh. "You weren't hallucinating—you were having a vision."

"A vision? Like, seeing the future kind of vision?"

He nodded, and I stared at him. The man was officially off his rocker. I knew seers existed, but they were rare, and there was no way I was one. I'd been having seizures with hallucinations my entire life. If they'd been visions, we would have figured that out a long time ago. Of course, the last few had been more coherent than they had ever been before, but that was just a fluke … right?

"I can't be … they're not … you're wrong."

"Not about this," he replied.

"Yeah, well, what makes you think I'm a seer?"

"For starters, normal humans don't get familiars, but seers do. Seers need their familiar to help channel their magic, or it will disperse throughout their body, causing convulsions and other symptoms."

My jaw worked as I digested what he said. "Seizures."

He nodded. "Many seers don't show signs of their power

until after they bond with their familiar. But some, like you, start having visions early. Unfortunately, without a familiar, they're so fractured they're useless."

Fractured ... that was a good way to explain them. What he said made a horrible kind of sense, but I still wasn't convinced *I* was a seer.

"I've been having seizures since I was five," I protested. "Surely by now someone would have noticed if I was a seer."

He shrugged. "Not necessarily. Most of what I know comes from a book I read *after* meeting you."

"A book?" I perked up a little. Maybe if I read the book too, I could figure out why he was so insistent that I was a seer.

He nodded. "I suspected something after you had that ... episode ... the day we met, so I went home and did some research."

I remembered that seizure and the knot on my head from him not catching me when I fell. I also remembered him telling me my seizure medication was useless. If he was right, it would explain why I had so much trouble finding one that worked. I guess we'd figure it out soon enough—I didn't have any with me, and I doubted Agent Stone would let me go back and get some.

"So, I had a seizure and you went 'yeah, she's a seer?'"

"Well, your eyes glowed too, so that was a pretty good indicator that something magical was happening."

I stared at him. "My eyes what?"

But apparently, he was done talking because he walked over to his pack and rooted around until he pulled out a book. He tossed it to me, and I caught it. He settled down in his corner of the cave and left me to read. I glanced at the cover. *Seers, As We Know Them.* He must have been confident about his conclusion to so casually give me this book, though I couldn't figure out *why* he'd give it to me. Surely, keeping me ignorant would suit his plans better.

With one eye on the agent, I quietly let Chrys out of the cage, scooping her bowl into my lap before settling back with the book. Situated as we were at the back of the cave, I had to squint to make out the words on the page. It didn't take long for my exhaustion and the low light to catch up to me. My eyelids drooped, and the words on the page blurred.

Chapter 32

Miriam

I JERKED AWAKE when Agent Stone sprang to his feet, his gun appearing in his hand as if by magic. In the silence of the cave, the sound of it cocking was deafening. My heart pounded in my ears, and I shrank back into my little corner.

"Jason! Let Miriam go!" The voice, though strong and angry, wrapped me in a cocoon of safety, and I nearly sobbed in relief.

He's here. He found me. Everything will be fine now. I couldn't explain why I believed that. Logically, Agent Stone had the upper hand over Lucas in every conceivable way.

"Lucas?" Agent Stone seemed thrown off by his presence. "What are you doing here? How did you find me? You need to leave—it's not safe. The seer stays with me."

"No."

It was a single word, but filled with such power that it was a tangible weight against my skin. I wanted to sink into it and wrap it around myself—it was safety, and freedom, and comfort.

The ground beneath us trembled, and thick vines shot out, wrapping around the SAID agent, pinning his arms to his side. I stared in shock—such a display of power was nearly unheard of. Even more shockingly, that power felt like *Lucas*—I was sure of it.

"Miriam?" he called.

"Here," I replied, my voice trembling as I poked my head out of my hiding spot.

Lucas was at my side in an instant, pulling me and Chrys into his arms. I buried my face in his chest as I sobbed. Once again, this incredible man had come to my rescue when I needed him most. I didn't know what I'd done to deserve him, but I'd spend the rest of our days together making sure he knew how much I appreciated and loved him.

Click.

"Really, Dylan? Pictures? Now?"

"It's for posterity," a familiar deep voice replied.

I looked over, expecting to find him taking pictures of Lucas and me. Instead, I found Agent Blazewing posing for pictures beside the trussed-up Agent Stone. I stared at him in confusion.

"How did the two of you end up here ... together?" I asked. I'd thought for sure that I'd die alone in the desert, my body never found.

"That's all Lucas," Agent Blazewing said before posing for another picture. "He tapped into your connection. Tracked you all the way here."

Connection?

I looked at Lucas in confusion.

He shrugged sheepishly. "I'll explain at home."

Home. That sounded good to me.

"No!" Agent Stone shouted. "You can't take her back—she isn't safe there! I need to take her away—"

The vines wrapping him grew, snaking around his mouth, cutting him off.

"You aren't taking her anywhere," Lucas growled. "No one is taking her anywhere she doesn't wish to go."

Somebody bring a mop because I'm a puddle.

"Get them out of here," Dylan said with a jerk of his head towards the cave entrance.

Lucas ushered us out as Chrys trilled happily. I looked down to find a second teacup griffin curled around Chrys, his dark blue-gray fur a striking contrast to her cream-colored coat.

Aw, Chrys found her mate. I didn't know how I was so certain about that, but I was. I looked up at Lucas. *And maybe I found mine.* I mentally shook myself. *No. No. No. That's the trauma talking. Lucas is fantastic, and definitely worth getting to know better, but thinking of marrying someone you've known for less than a week is just crazy. Cool your jets, or you'll scare him off. He'd make a handsome groom, though.*

"I can't believe he cuffed you—I'm gonna kill him," Lucas muttered when he caught sight of my still-cuffed hands. "Let me try something."

He gestured for me to sit, and a slender vine snaked out of the ground and slid into the lock. A few seconds later, the handcuffs clinked to the ground.

Chrys shrieked, and a familiar pressure built in my chest.

"Caramel apple pie bars," I blurted out. *What is with me randomly shouting about food? Great. Now I'm hungry ... -er, hungrier.*

"Caramel ... apple?" Lucas looked at me quizzically.

"I ... I'm sorry. I don't know why I said that. I've never had that before or knew it existed. I mean, I know apple pie exists, and I've had some, and I'm sure some people put caramel on it, but I don't even know if pie bars are a thing. If they're not, they should be, but I'm not sure where it came from. And now I'm babbling. I-I must be hungry."

Lucas chuckled. "Apple pie bars are most definitely a thing—they're my mom's specialty. One of them, anyway. Unfortunately, I didn't bring any food with me, but I promise we'll stop for some when we reach civilization again, even if it is fast food." His nose wrinkled, and his brows pinched together as if the thought was physically painful.

I snickered. "You mean you didn't pack a twelve-course meal before haring off on a dangerous rescue mission? That's like, basic supplies."

He nodded. "An oversight, to be sure."

"If I promise not to perish of hunger on the way back, would you make me a sandwich or something when we get home?"

He smiled broadly, his green eyes lighting up. "I'm going to kiss you now," he said.

And he did. Any further thoughts about food perished the moment his lips touched mine.

Chapter 33

Lucas

CLICK.

I broke off the kiss and turned to glare at my friend, who stood unabashedly taking pictures of us.

"For posterity," he said with a cheeky grin.

Miriam blushed in my arms.

"Anyways," Dylan continued as he held up a pair of keys, "I'm going to check Jason's car to see if he has any magic-dampening cuffs. If he does, we can secure him and get out of here. Otherwise, we'll have to wait for backup."

"And you had to interrupt us to tell us that because …? You couldn't have just checked on your own?"

Dylan grinned. "Because this way was more fun."

I sighed and looked at Miriam. "I'm sorry. My friends are the worst. One former friend kidnaps you, and the other—"

"Wait, what?" Miriam looked at me in alarm. "Agent Stone was one of your friends?"

I grimaced. *"Was."* I took a deep breath. "Remember how I

said I was staging an intervention for one of my friends?"

Miriam nodded.

"Jason was that friend. If I'd known he planned on kidnapping you, I would have made him foxglove tea instead."

Her lips twitched. "Sounds like a tea party to die for."

Stars above, I love this woman. And I showed it by kissing her again.

Dylan muttered in confusion as he walked off to Jason's car. He returned a few minutes later, a pair of cuffs in his hands.

"Romeo, I need you to release Jason so I can cuff him."

"Not Romeo. Never Romeo—he's an idiot," I said.

Miriam laughed.

Dylan rolled his eyes. "Fine. Just get in there and help me out. We can't leave him here."

"That's your opinion," I replied, even as I moved to help him. I paused, then turned back to give Miriam a kiss on the cheek. "I'll be right back."

I re-entered the cave, and Canterbury's tiny weight settled on my shoulder. I didn't want to release Jason—Miriam would be safer if he stayed here, forever, but leaving him to rot would be wrong.

"Try freeing just his hands first."

I nodded at Dylan and turned my focus to the thick vines encasing Jason. I reached out with my senses and prodded the magic in them, but they wouldn't budge. I pushed and pulled, but nothing. I yanked with all my might, and with a *snap* that I felt more than heard, the magic sprang from where it had been trapped in the vines and pummeled me, digging into my skin as it sought to return to me.

A scream rang in my ears, and the dim cave grew dark. Canterbury shrieked as up became down, and my face hit something hard and unforgiving. I tasted dirt, heavy with the tang of iron.

***

I peeled my eyes open, feeling like someone had attached weights to my eyelids. I caught a brief flash of the interior of a car before my eyes fell shut again. I didn't have the strength to reopen them. My head pounded, every vein and muscle burned, and my stomach churned. Something chirped at me from somewhere near my chest. A cool, gentle hand stroked my forehead. An angelic voice murmured something, but I couldn't make out the words. Eventually, I scraped together the strength to reach up and capture the hand, holding onto it like a lifeline as I drifted off again. I didn't know where I was or what was happening. I barely remembered my own name. The only thing I was certain of was that as long as I held onto that hand, everything would be fine.

Chapter 34

Miriam

I STARED AFTER LUCAS, an unsettled feeling in my gut. I wanted to call him back and make him stay beside me, but I didn't.

Seconds dragged into minutes. Then a scream rang out, shattering the stillness of the desert. My heart stopped. I knew that scream, though I'd never heard it before.

"Lucas!" I shouted as I sprinted to the cave, getting bowled over by a mass of feathers and fur. I scrambled to my feet and watched as an eerily familiar griffin winged away. *Just like the one in my dream.*

There was no time to think about that, though. I turned back to the cave entrance and ran inside.

Lucas sprawled out on the cave floor, deathly still, surrounded by gray dust. Agent Blazewing knelt at his side, checking his pulse.

"He's breathing, but barely. We need to get him to the hospital."

He scooped Lucas into his arms and strode out of the cave.

I followed behind, feeling utterly useless and lost.

"What happened? Did Agent Stone do this?" I demanded.

"I don't know," Agent Blazewing said. "I don't think Jason … Stone would do this." He paused. "But if he is responsible, I'll kill him myself," he muttered so quietly I almost didn't hear him.

I climbed into Agent Stone's vehicle first, once again in the backseat. I deposited Chrys' bowl in the center console between the driver and passenger seat—she'd be safe enough there for the ride. Agent Blazewing passed Lucas to me, and together we situated him in the backseat with his head on my lap. He was so tall that his legs dangled off the seat at an awkward angle.

"Keep an eye on his breathing. If he stops, yell." With that, the agent slammed the door shut and climbed into the front seat.

Lucas' familiar fluttered over and settled on his chest.

We tore across the desert, sirens blaring and a dust cloud blooming behind us. We jostled to and fro with every bump in the path, and it took all of my strength to keep Lucas on the seat with me. I prayed to every god I believed in and even ones I didn't. Lucas' breath remained shallow and erratic.

We hit the main road with a bump and sped down the highway, cars parting before us. Dylan pulled a radio out from somewhere and demanded directions to the nearest hospital. A few incomprehensible sentences followed, and Dylan gruffly thanked the person on the other end.

Lucas' eyes fluttered open for the briefest moment, and a flicker of hope lit in my chest. I stroked his forehead, wishing I could do more than sit there and hold him.

"Stay with me, Lucas. Please stay with me. I can't lose you."

His hand reached out and grabbed mine, holding onto it tightly. The strength of his grip was reassuring—if he had the strength to hold onto my hand like that, surely, he had the strength to survive this.

A few minutes later, we pulled into the emergency lane in front of a hospital. I didn't know where we were, but I knew it wasn't Wellspring. A team of nurses and doctors were already waiting for Lucas. They loaded him onto a gurney with brisk efficiency, only hampered by the fact that he wouldn't let go of my hand.

One of the nurses tried prying us apart, and even though I relaxed my grip so they could take him, his grip tightened. Eventually, they gave up and ushered me into the hospital alongside Lucas, leaving Agent Blazewing behind. I looked over my shoulder in time to catch the anguished expression on his face before the doors closed behind us.

They peppered me with questions while they took Lucas' vitals. They didn't like what they found out from either of us.

"You believe he was trying to work magic, and then he collapsed? But you didn't see it yourself?" a doctor clarified.

I'm sure he'd introduced himself at some point, but my mind was a jumbled mess. The only thing that was clear was that Lucas was in danger.

I nodded. "I was outside the cave. I ran in when I heard him scream. By the time I got there, he was already unconscious."

The doctor thought for a moment, then ordered a slew of tests. I tried to stay out of the way as best as possible, but with

Lucas refusing to let go of my hand, I was always a little underfoot.

"Sorry," I apologized as a nurse had to yet again walk around me to do their job.

The doctors didn't seem to like the results of the tests because more kept coming. They even put Lucas inside a giant tubular machine, and I had to stand awkwardly leaning half inside it. Even with the strain, Lucas' grip never faltered.

Finally, the barrage of tests was done, and we quietly waited in a room for the results. They'd hooked Lucas up to numerous machines and IV fluids. I rested my head on his arm, silently begging him to just wake up.

The door opened, and I looked up, expecting a doctor, but it was Agent Blazewing with our familiars. Lucas' flew out of the nest and landed on his chest, where he curled up and tucked his head under a wing.

"Named him Canterbury," the agent said with a nod to the blue and gray teacup griffin.

I let out a strangled half-sob. "How much you want to bet that's after a plant, not the book?"

His lips twitched. "That's a pretty safe bet. Lucas always did love his plants."

"Did you know Lucas before this … disaster?"

"Yeah," he said as he pulled up a chair next to me. "We were roommates in college. He's one of my best friends, and one of the greatest men I know. How did you two meet?"

"We met at the train station when our bus left without us. We walked together for a little bit, then he invited me to one of his lectures."

"And that worked?"

"Not really. A gremlin derailed my return train, and I had nothing else to do, so I figured, why not? Anyways, he asked me out after the lecture, and that was that."

"Cute."

"Hmm."

I couldn't help but feel that this was all my fault. If I'd never met Lucas, he wouldn't be in the hospital right now.

"This isn't your fault," Agent Blazewing said. "It isn't your fault you were kidnapped, and it certainly isn't your fault that Lucas came to rescue you. That was *his* decision. We tried to stop him, what with his recent hospitalization—"

"His what?!"

"Ah, right. You wouldn't know. Lucas saw Jason kidnap you. He tried to stop Jason but ended up in the ER for his troubles."

"I … I don't remember that." I felt guilty. Shouldn't I remember my boyfriend trying to rescue me? I remembered unlocking the door, thinking it was Lucas, but not much after that.

"I'm not surprised. Lucas said you were having a seizure … a vision, I suppose."

I snorted.

"You doubt it?"

I shrugged. "You don't?"

"Persimmon."

"I don't follow."

"In the shop. I was looking for clues to an exotic animal smuggling ring, and you told me 'persimmon.'" He nodded towards Canterbury. "I found them on Persimmon Lane. Your prediction was the break I needed in the case."

"That ... that doesn't prove anything."

"Did you stop to wonder why Lucas has such strong magic? Normally, not even full elves can do what he did in the cave."

I hadn't. I didn't know much about magic, a fact that was becoming increasingly obvious.

"Every seer has a guardian, a familiar, and a focus," he continued. "A familiar helps the seer channel the magic. The focus helps control and clarify. And the guardian, well, guards."

I looked at Lucas, and my heart ached as I thought of the implications. "You think Lucas is my guardian?"

Agent Blazewing nodded. "He's done things with magic in the last day that I never thought possible—and it all surrounds you. Every great act of magic had you at the center."

"Did I do that to him? Did I make him a guardian without his consent?" I wouldn't be able to live with myself if I forced Lucas into a role he never asked for. If that was the case, how would this *not* be my fault? And would Lucas ever forgive me?

"Mmm ... I don't think so, but my knowledge of seers comes because of a college essay. Sorry. This might help, though." He reached into his coat pocket and passed over a familiar book. "Found this in the cave. Thought it might be useful. I'm guessing it was Jason's. Coincidentally, it's the same one I read for my essay years ago."

I took it with a nod of thanks, but I didn't bother opening it. The last thing I wanted to do right now was read anything that had to do with Jason. And even if I had wanted to read it right then, my mind felt overstuffed and wrung out—I wouldn't be able to focus on anything.

Chapter 35

Miriam

I SNAPPED AWAKE when the doctor cleared her throat. She was vaguely familiar, and I couldn't tell if it was because she was one of the doctors from before or because I was terrible with faces and just couldn't tell the doctors apart. I struggled to read her name tag, but my eyes wouldn't focus. Lucas was still unconscious and holding my hand—I didn't think I would be getting it back any time soon.

"I'm sorry, could you repeat that?" I asked.

"We believe Mr. Fernleaf to be suffering from magical burnout. He tried to channel too much magic that wasn't his own, and it burned him from the inside, in a manner of speaking."

That sounds really, really bad.

"What ... what can we do for him?"

"We have some medication to give him intravenously. The medicine will help his body repair his magic channels. I won't lie though, whether or not he pulls through is up to him."

After giving Lucas his medicine, the doctor monitored him

for a few minutes and then left.

Magical burnout. Just what was he doing that caused this?

"Agent Blazewing, how … how did Lucas burn himself with magic? Just how much was he trying to channel?"

It didn't make sense. After what I'd seen him do, tying Agent Stone up as if it was nothing, releasing him should have been a drop in the bucket compared to that.

"Dylan. You're Lucas' girl—you're practically family. Hearing you call me 'Agent' is a little weird at this point."

I raised an eyebrow pointedly. He hadn't answered my question.

He sighed. "I'm not sure it was the *amount* of magic that did it. If I had to bet, I'd say it had more to do with him being a guardian."

"He burned out *because* he's my guardian?" That thought made me even more heartsick than thinking I'd accidentally forced him into the role of a guardian.

"Not exactly. As a guardian, the purpose of his magic is to protect you. If he thought what he was doing put you in jeopardy, it's possible he suffered some sort of magical backlash from it."

I sat with that thought for a few minutes, but it didn't make a difference. It all boiled down to one fact: Lucas was hurt because of me.

Dylan's phone beeped, and his eyebrows rose in surprise when he read the text. "So … how do you feel about meeting the parents?"

"Your parents? Why would I care about meeting them?" I

paused as I processed what I'd said. "Sorry. That was rude."

Dylan snickered. "Tell me how you really feel. No, I meant Lucas' parents. But, for the record, mine are awesome."

I jerked in my chair and turned to look at him. "Are you telling me that Lucas' parents are on their way?"

"His parents, siblings, their familiars … the whole family is descending on this hospital en mass."

"When?"

"About five minutes."

I took a panicked breath. "So soon? I was under the impression that they lived a few states away."

"They do. Apparently, Nolan called them when Lucas ran off with a SAID team. I'm not sure if he was trying to recruit reinforcements or just tattle on him. Either way, they all hopped on the first flight to Phoenix, then hightailed it out here when they heard about Lucas."

"Fantastic." I looked around the hospital room, but it was bereft of suitable hiding places.

He chuckled. "Don't panic. They're great people—they'll love you."

"You know, that doesn't actually help."

Meeting the parents would be nerve-wracking enough on a normal day, but in this situation? I was the reason their son (who I'd only been dating for a few days) was in the hospital. I wouldn't be surprised if I was *persona non grata.*

The next few minutes seemed to stretch into eternity as I kept my eyes glued on the door. Then, a sound. But not from where I expected.

Chapter 36

Lucas

MY HEAD THROBBED IN TIME TO THE BEEPING NEARBY. *Stupid alarm clock.* I opened my eyes— they were dry and gritty. I tried to rub them but only succeeded in smacking myself in the face. I grunted. *Behold my grace.*

"Lucas?"

I turned my head slightly, and my muscles protested. I wasn't in my room at all. Miriam sat at my bedside, her chair pulled up close, her hand tucked into mine. The dark bags under her eyes spoke of exhaustion. Her hair haloed her face in wild curls. *There has to be a better way than getting hospitalized to see her first thing when I wake up.*

"Hey, beautiful," I said.

"Hey, handsome. How are you feeling?"

"Like I got chewed up and spat out by a dragon."

"Well, you tasted terrible," my friend piped in.

Up near my head, Canterbury chirped. Somewhere off to my right, Chrys responded.

"And where did you learn the phrase 'death warmed over?'" I asked my familiar. That was by far the clearest message I'd ever gotten from him.

Miriam grinned as she reached up to brush a strand of hair out of my face. "Probably from Agent Blazewing."

I grunted. "Figures. I bet that was his nicest phrase for me."

Miriam nodded.

"You're not wrong," Dylan said.

"What happened?" I asked.

"The doctors said that magic burned you. They said you overreached and tried to use magic that wasn't yours." She sounded dubious, almost hesitant.

"But ...?"

"Agent Blazewing has a different theory. Something about the magic rebelling because what you asked of it was against its nature ... against *your* nature."

"But ...?"

"But that theory only holds water if ... if I'm a seer, and you're my ... my guardian."

"Dylan told you?"

She shook her head. "Agent Stone did first, then Agent Blazewing ... Dylan."

"But you don't believe them."

"It doesn't really matter right now. All that matters is making sure you recover."

She was deflecting, and we both knew it. She'd have to

come to terms with her seership on her own, just like I had to come to terms with my guardianship. And what a poor excuse for a guardian I was. I'd not only lost her, but when I went to rescue her, I'd ended up needing to be rescued myself. If Jason hadn't been tied up already, I might have lost her again. *Speaking of* ...

"What happened to Jason?"

"Agent Stone? He ... he escaped."

"What?!" I exclaimed, jerking upright, and every muscle screamed in agony. I flopped back down on the bed. "What happened?"

"When you collapsed, the vines desiccated. Agent Stone used the distraction to escape."

I groaned. He got away again, and once again, it was all my fault.

As if sensing my thoughts, Miriam leaned over and rested her forehead against mine. "None of this is your fault, Lucas. No one blames you. Without you, no one would have even *thought* to look for me. You're my hero Lucas."

Tears pricked my eyes, and I brought my free hand up to cup her face. "Sorry I let the villain get away."

"You saved me, if that's any consolation."

"Angel, you are no consolation prize. You are everything."

She sniffed, tears running down her face. "That's not fair. You don't get to be charming, romantic, *and* handsome while lying in a hospital bed after nearly dying rescuing me. There has to be something wrong with you."

"He snores," an unexpected voice piped up.

I closed my eyes. *This isn't happening. They're not here. You're just imagining this.*

"His feet smell," another added.

"He makes Dad jokes," a third said.

"He *laughs* at Dad jokes," a fourth replied.

"Hush, all of you," another chided. "This is not the time to be roasting your brother."

"You're right," the first said. "The magic already did that."

Smack.

"Ow! Sorry Lucas. I shouldn't have said that."

I opened my eyes. *Dang. It didn't work.* My family was most definitely here.

My small hospital room suddenly felt very crowded. Dad towered over everyone while Mom's short frame put her barely a head and shoulders above the hospital bed.

"How are you feeling, Son?" Dad asked while Mom moved around to pile tubs of food onto my bedside tray.

"Like a pig at a luau?" Jonas, my younger brother, suggested.

Smack. Jonas grimaced and rubbed the back of his head ruefully but didn't take his words back. I didn't see who smacked him, but I was betting it was Azalea. She glared at Jonas, her arms now crossed, and her fairy squirrel perched on her shoulder, mimicking her pose.

"Pretty much, yeah. But I promise I don't taste as good."

Jonas visibly restrained himself from making another smart-aleck response. His amphithere curled around his neck and nuzzled his jaw, either consoling him or congratulating him on his self-control.

"When did you guys get here?"

"Like ten seconds ago," Orchid said. She turned to Miriam. "If you need embarrassing stories about him, ask Azalea—she's got oodles. For pictures, ask Mom."

"No! She doesn't need those! Thank you, but I'd actually like to *not* scare her off."

"Well, she stuck around with you looking like *that*, so I don't think there's any danger," Jonas pointed out.

That earned him another smack from Azalea.

I sighed. "The mouthy one is my brother, Jonas. My mom, Hester, is arranging a five-course meal on the bedside table. My dad, Birch, is the tall one. Azalea's the one with the fairy squirrel. Orchid's wearing the blue shirt. Iris is wearing green."

"It's not a five-course meal." Mom tsked. "Just a few caramel apple pie bars to get you through."

"Mmmm. Caramel apple pie bars, didn't *see* that one coming."

Miriam flashed me a panicked look, and I backed off. If she wasn't ready to discuss this, then I wouldn't push.

The door opened, and a nurse poked her head in. "I'm sorry. I know you're all very concerned, but only two visitors per room. I'm going to have to ask some of you to leave and take turns visiting."

My siblings grumbled but dutifully filed out of the room, with Dylan close on their heels. Miriam squeezed my hand and leaned forward to kiss my forehead.

"I'll be right out there if you need me," she whispered, then slipped her hand out of mine and stepped away.

I felt her absence like a yawning chasm that threatened to swallow me whole. Darkness crept in at the edges of my vision, and my eyelids drooped. A heavy weight settled on my chest. Beside me, machines blared in alarm. Sounds grew muffled as though I was underwater. I was dimly aware of some commotion. Then, a soft hand slipped into mine, and the world was right again.

"Lucas, you with us?" the doctor asked.

I nodded, though it took some effort. "Yeah. What happened?"

"That's what I'd like to find out," she replied. "I'm Dr. Kamirsa. Hang in there with me—I want to test something."

Without warning, Miriam's hand was ripped from me, and the chasm opened once again. Darkness encroached, and machines blared. Then her hand settled in mine again, and the chasm closed, and the machines settled.

I took a few deep breaths, and again, her hand was taken. Again, the chasm opened. This time, when her hand returned, I clasped onto it like a lifeline.

"No more," I begged. "No more."

Darkness claimed me.

Chapter 37

Miriam

I SAT AT LUCAS' BEDSIDE, holding his hand, afraid to let go. Every time I stepped away, his heart beat erratically, and machines blared, summoning a herd of doctors and nurses from the ether. Then, like magic, when I held his hand, he stabilized. I felt like a human pacemaker. I had to flag down a doctor every time I needed to use the restroom.

I didn't understand why it happened, and neither did the doctors. They'd called a specialist in magical burnout from halfway across the country, but they wouldn't get here until tomorrow. I glanced down at my phone. Today, then.

Lucas' family had left a long time ago when visiting hours ended, but his mom left us with an entire container of caramel apple pie bars. I tried telling myself that it was just a coincidence, that I wasn't really a seer, but too many things were adding up. In the end, I thanked Lucas' mom for the treat and nibbled on a square to be polite. Before I realized it, I'd already eaten half of the container. Lucas had gamely eaten a few bites, but that was all he had the energy for. That, more than all the wires sticking from him, had worried his mom.

My eyes were gritty from exhaustion, and these hospital chairs were not designed with comfort in mind. I twisted in my seat, but no amount of stretching would make the backache go away. The lack of sleep was catching up to me, and I looked over at Chrys and Canterbury enviously.

"Hey," Lucas said softly, "you need to get some sleep."

"I can't leave you."

He chuckled. "You don't have to. These beds are big enough for both of us."

He scooted over as best as he could, which was probably only an inch or so, but I climbed up next to him anyway. It took a bit of awkward shuffling, but eventually we were situated as comfortably as possible.

"Hmm, not really how I imagined our first sleepover going," Lucas mumbled sleepily.

I snorted. It turned into a snicker, which turned into full-blown laughter, the kind of laughter that happens in the wee hours of the morning when exhaustion makes everything funny.

"Lucas," I gasped between bouts of laughter, "you can't say stuff like that."

"Hmm, insert smart rebuttal here," he replied.

I buried my face in his shoulder, trying to stifle the laughter. "You can't do that! That's cheating! You actually have to come up with a response."

"Maybe that *was* my response."

"Shush, you." I covered his mouth with my free hand. "I'm way too tired to sensibly deal with your nonsense."

He kissed the palm of my hand. "Goodnight, princess."

"Goodnight, my knight in leafy armor."

I drifted off, and if the doctors or nurses checked on us throughout the night, I had no recollection of it.

***

"Aww, they're so cute!"

"Shh! Don't wake them up!"

I cracked an eye open to see Lucas' two younger sisters standing in the doorway, one of them with her phone out, taking pictures. *Iris ... or is it Orchid? Not Azalea—she has the fairy squirrel.* I moved to sit up, but Lucas' arm tightened around me.

"If we ignore them, they might leave," he stage-whispered.

"Rude! Just for that, we'll let you eat the nasty hospital breakfast," the taller of the two said, waving a couple boxes.

Lucas sat up, grimacing in pain. "Hey now, no need for threats. We're all family here."

"Mom packed some for you too, Miriam," the shorter said. "We also brought you a change of clothes."

She held up a reusable shopping bag. I wondered where she'd gotten the clothing from, as the bag I'd packed for Lucas' was sitting under the chair next to the hospital bed. Once Lucas had stabilized yesterday, Dylan had been kind enough to drive all the way back to Wellspring to grab the bag so I could feed the teacup griffins and give Chrys her medicine.

"Thank you ..." I paused.

"Iris," she supplied.

"Iris," I said, committing her face to memory.

She was shorter than Orchid and Azalea. Like the rest of her siblings, she had red hair, but hers was more strawberry blonde, whereas Orchid's curls looked like gleaming copper.

I accepted the bag gratefully. *Maybe I can go change when the doctor comes to check on Lucas.*

I scooted off the bed and repositioned myself in the chair. Lucas squeezed my hand.

"I'll be fine for a few minutes if you want to go change and freshen up," he said.

I pegged him with a look. "I appreciate the offer, but I'm not leaving you to code without a doctor nearby, and certainly not while there's delicious food to eat."

My stomach gave a well-timed rumble.

"Priorities," Orchid said approvingly.

"Alright, what's on the menu this morning?" Lucas asked.

"Stuffed French toast cinnamon roll bites with buttermilk syrup, maple sausage links, scrambled eggs, and a side of fresh fruit," Orchid said as she presented the boxes with a flourish. "All of it bite-size for the invalid." She set the boxes on the bedtable and patted Lucas' cheek condescendingly.

Lucas batted her hand away and then pushed one of the boxes closer to me while Orchid passed out the forks.

Whatever a Stuffed French Toast Cinnamon Roll was, it smelled heavenly. I opened the box and nearly drooled. I wasted no time and very little manners on scarfing it down. Lucas managed about a third of his box, which was more than he'd managed all of yesterday.

Canterbury fluttered up to Lucas' food and stole a raspberry that was nearly as big as his head. He proudly took his spoils back to Chrys, and the two enjoyed their breakfast. I grimaced at the mess they made as they ate.

There was a knock on the door, and Orchid and Iris traded places with Jonas and Azalea. Azalea brought me a book, and Jonas brought his questionable sense of humor.

"So, Miriam, when are you going to dump this loser and go out with me?" He winked and struck an outrageous pose.

"The thirty-sixth of November," I quipped.

He paused and stared at me while Lucas laughed. "That ... that wasn't supposed to work."

Azalea smacked him upside the head. "It didn't dumb-dumb. November doesn't *have* thirty-six days."

"Oh ... right ... good." He shrugged. "It wouldn't have worked between us anyway—I can't date someone stupid enough to break Lucas' heart. You know, bro code and all that."

Lucas wiped away an imaginary tear. "That's the nicest thing you've ever said to me."

"Eh, don't get used to it."

A loud shriek interrupted us, and we all turned to see Jonas' amphithere busy trying to insert himself into Chrys' nest.

"Clarence, what in the world are you doing?" Jonas asked his familiar. "Did you *ask* if they wanted you to egg-sit?"

Clarence hung his head, looking dejected as he slid out of

the nest.

"Dude, we gotta get you a girlfriend." He paused. "We gotta get *me* a girlfriend." He looked at me. "Got any sisters?"

"No. Only child, sorry."

He shrugged. "Worth a shot."

A knock on the door signaled the end of their visit.

Chapter 38

Lucas

ZALEA AND JONAS LEFT, letting Mom and Dad in behind them. With Miriam keeping me alive, the doctor decided she didn't count as a visitor, so I could have two other people as well.

"Hi, Mom. Thanks for breakfast."

"Morning, Son. How are you feeling today?" She glanced at my partially-eaten breakfast and frowned slightly.

"Better than yesterday," I replied.

"You've got us right worried," Dad said.

"I know. I'm sorry."

"Don't be. Dylan told us what you did. We're right proud of the man you've become. Just take care of yourself and Miriam, you hear?"

Dad was laconic—from him, that was practically an entire speech.

"I will, Dad."

"So," Mom said as she sat down in the other chair and made

herself comfortable, "Miriam, tell us about yourself. Other than telling us you exist, Lucas has been sparing on the details."

Thankfully, she didn't mention the phone call where we cooked up a scheme where I'd pretend to need Miriam's kitchen and leave her a boatload of food in payment. A scheme that I'd had to put on hold when she came to stay at my place.

"Oh," Miriam said, and I could see her shrink in on herself. "I work at a local bookshop in Wellspring, and um … I like to read."

When it became obvious that she wasn't going to say more, Mom reached over and squeezed Miriam's hand. "My dear, you are far more than just your job and a single hobby. I've only known you a few hours, but I can tell you're something special. And one day, I hope you'll know it too."

Miriam blinked back a few tears and nodded.

I reached over with my free hand and gently brushed her face. "Mom's right. You're kind, and brave, and loyal. You have a smile that lights up the room and a witty sense of humor. And that is just the tip of the iceberg."

She was crying now, and I wanted nothing more than to pull her into my arms and kiss her until the tears stopped.

"Food service," a chipper voice said from the doorway. An orderly with a food tray stood there, smiling brightly. "I see you've already had breakfast. Would you like me to leave this tray or take it with me?"

"You can take it, thank you."

As he left, a pair of doctors entered. One was Dr. Kamirsa from yesterday. From the bags under her eyes, I hoped her shift was almost over and she could go to sleep. The other doctor was studying something on their tablet.

"Mr. Fernleaf, it's good to see you awake. This is Dr. Stevensen, an expert in magical burnout. They will be consulting on your case."

Mom and Dad quietly excused themselves to give us privacy.

Dr. Stevensen looked up and smiled. "It's good to meet you. Would you prefer Lucas or Mr. Fernleaf?"

"Lucas, please. Only my students call me Mr. Fernleaf."

"You're a teacher?"

"A professor of botany and soil sciences."

They raised an eyebrow. "Impressive. And this must be Miriam. I hear we have her to thank for you still being around."

I nodded. "Can't complain about holding my beautiful girlfriend's hand all day, but I'd like to know *why* this is happening. And I'm sure Miriam would like to *not* be my life-support sometime soon."

"Fair enough. You're a unique case, Lucas." They flipped their tablet around to show me something on the screen. "This is an image from the MCS[7] we ran on you. See these black spidery veins here?"

I nodded.

"These show significant burns in your magic channels." They flipped through several more images, all showing black

---

[7] MCS: Magic Channel Scan (literally a scan of a person's magic channels)

veining. "As you can see, the burnout is quite significant throughout your entire body, except for here." They flipped to a final image, one of my hand entwined with Miriam's. Her hand, a human hand, glowed with golden veins as thin as spider silk. Glowing golden veins crawled up my arm from where her hand held mine. A glance at Miriam convinced me it was not the time to point out that ordinary humans wouldn't have magic channels at all.

"It appears that your girlfriend is somehow reversing the effects of your magical burnout. I'd like to run another MCS and see where we stand this morning."

I agreed and was soon being wheeled out of the room with Miriam walking beside me. The doctors must have anticipated my agreement and booked the room ahead of time. We passed my family milling in the hallway.

"Just going for a quick test," I reassured them.

"You'll be fine," Jonas said. "You've always been great at tests."

I'd been unconscious during my only previous MCS so I didn't know what to expect. It turned out to involve stuffing me inside a long tube with Miriam awkwardly reaching inside the tube while still holding my hand. I was going to spend a long time making it up to her for all of this. Not for the first time, I wished I'd told Dylan to stuff it and that Jonas could rot in the cave until someone came with heavy-duty pruning shears, or maybe a chainsaw.

It felt like the scan lasted forever, but it was probably closer to half an hour. Then we were shuffled off to my room to await the results.

"How'd it go?" Azalea asked as we passed my passel of relatives.

I shook my head. "Can't say. I forgot to study—just marked 'C' on everything."

"Hey! That's what I did! Ironically, that was also my grade," Jonas joked.

"At least his sense of humor is intact," Orchid muttered.

I nodded as I patted my elbow. "Yep. X-rays confirm—no damage to the funny bone."

My sisters rolled their eyes, and Miriam snickered. I flashed her a smile and squeezed her hand.

Miriam stopped the doctors before they left so they could watch me while she used the restroom. I felt a bit like a baby being passed off, but I could hardly complain about her needing a bathroom break.

Her hand slipped from mine, and it felt like I was suddenly trying to breathe through a straw. A machine beeped. One of the doctors slipped an oxygen mask over my face, and the encroaching darkness retreated.

"Lucas," Dr. Stevensen said, "tell us how you're feeling."

"Better than yesterday," I replied. "I don't feel like there's an elephant on my chest, but breathing is a bit hard. Yesterday, every time Miriam let go of my hand, I felt like there was this big, dark, bottomless pit ready to swallow me up. That feeling is mostly gone, but if I'd been standing up, I would have needed to sit down. I'm a little dizzy."

"Hmm. Your heart rate's keeping steady, which is good to see. The dizziness and other symptoms could be due to lack of oxygen—your O2 levels took a dip when your girlfriend left. The progress is heartening, but we'll keep monitoring you."

Miriam came back wearing a new white dress with a colorful floral print and a relieved expression. "Hey, you're looking better than I expected."

"Yes! I got an 'exceeds expectations.'"

She laughed and kissed my forehead before slipping her hand back into mine. I took a deep breath, then coughed a little when the dry oxygen hit my lungs. I took the mask off and handed it back to Dr. Stevensen while Miriam passed me my water.

Chapter 39

Miriam

It was Wednesday morning, and Lucas was finally being released. They ran an MCS on him every day just to check his progress. While they were pleased with how he was improving, it wasn't until his oxygen stopped dropping every time I walked away that they finally agreed to consider releasing him.

His parents were driving us back to Wellspring in Lucas' truck. We'd ended up all the way down in Tucson, about an hour from Wellspring. I was grateful that this hospital had what Lucas needed, or he would have had to be life-flighted to another hospital, most likely without me.

It was a long drive home filled with awkward small talk between me and Lucas' mom. Lucas fell asleep after about ten minutes, and his father didn't seem prone to talking.

"So, what kind of books do you like to read?" she asked.

"A variety of fiction. I love regency romances, historical fiction, westerns, contemporary fiction, sci-fi, fantasy, … just about anything except horror and psychological thrillers."

"Jane Austen?"

"One of my favorite authors."

"There's a really popular cozy fiction that just came out about a magical baking competition, have you read it?"

I shook my head. "Not yet. I've got it on hold at the library. I think I'm twelfth in line, or something like that."

"You'll love it—it's an excellent book."

We spent the rest of the drive talking about books and food, which was great, but by the time we reached Wellspring, I was ready for some solitude.

"Would you mind dropping me off at my place? I'd like to shower."

"Of course, dear. Just give us a call if you want us to come pick you up."

They pulled into the parking lot of my apartment building, and Lucas woke up long enough to beg me to stay, and then say goodbye when I refused. Staying at my house probably wasn't a great idea, but I needed my space. Thankfully, Dylan had stationed one of his SAID agents outside the apartment, just in case Jason came back.

Chrys and Canterbury had their own tearful farewell, and I promised them that this separation wouldn't last.

I shuffled into my apartment and put Chrys on the counter before kicking off my shoes and dropping my bag unceremoniously on the floor. I gently stroked Chrys' head, mentally apologizing to her for having to reschedule her vet appointment. Hopefully soon we'd be able to take her bandages off. She was already walking around on occasion, and I was looking forward to seeing her fly. I set up her feeder beside her on the counter and shuffled off to the bathroom for a shower.

I stood under the shower head and let the hot water massage away the stress of the last few days. I washed my hair, too tired to be appalled at how much dirt ran down the drain with the soap. Soon, I was clean but nowhere near ready to get out. I sat with my back under the spray, wondering if there was enough hot water in the world to make me feel like myself again.

Me? A seer? Somebody had their wires crossed, and I doubted it was me. There wasn't always a magical explanation for something. Sometimes, a seizure was just a seizure.

I hadn't had a so-called vision in the last few days. Then again, I also hadn't had any of my seizure medication. Lucas had told me that Jason had probably switched out my regular meds for a placebo. I would have simply called my doctor to get a refill on the prescription, but I didn't have enough money in my account for the co-pay. I'd just have to make do until my paycheck, which would be smaller than normal because of the few days I'd had to take off. Even the extra hours I'd worked wouldn't be enough to cover that. I closed my eyes and hung my head. *Will life ever give me a break?*

I was just starting to relax when Chrys began a familiar shrieking. Heart pounding, I turned the water off and froze in indecision. Did the shrieking mean what I thought it meant, or was there some other danger? I forced myself to sit back in the tub for a few breaths. Just when I was about to give up and get out, the world fractured and slid away.

A familiar gravel path crunched under my feet as I sprinted. My breathing was ragged, and I clutched Chrys' bowl to my chest. The shadows behind me reached out, trying to grasp me in their oil-slick darkness. Lucas. I needed to get to Lucas.

Above me, a shadow circled and dove. A griffin landed in front of me, shifting in the blink of an eye. He raised a pistol.

"*I am not the enemy,*" *he said.*

BANG!

I came to with a gasp and sat upright, looking around wildly, but I was alone in my bathroom. Chrys was still making a racket, and I could feel her concern through our bond.

"I'm okay, Chrys!" I called out shakily. "I'll be right there!"

A few minutes later, with my hair still dripping wet, I sat on my kitchen floor with Chrys' bowl cradled in my lap.

"Thanks for warning me about the … seizure," I said.

Chrys gave me a disapproving look and chirped.

"Time to sneeze? Time … sneeze. Time sneeze. Vision? You're telling me these are actually visions?"

She chirped in affirmation.

No. No. No. This can't be. I can't be a seer. I don't want *to be a seer.* The terror some of those visions inspired was not something I ever wanted to experience in real life.

I could feel myself spiraling, and a soft head began stroking my thumb and purring. Of all the evidence placed before me, why was it my familiar that broke through my wall of denial?

My phone rang, and I answered it automatically.

"Hello?"

"Miriam! Are you okay?"

"Lucas? Yeah, I'm … no, I'm really not. I don't want to be a seer. Life was hard enough before … before all this. What if

I'm no good at this? What if I mess everything up? What if the rest of my life is nightmares and blurting things out at random times? What if you get hurt again because of me? What if you *die* because of me?"

I was ugly crying now, and in desperate need of a tissue. I had to pull myself together. The last thing Lucas needed right now was to have to deal with all of my issues too.

"What if?" Lucas repeated. "What if you end up being an incredible seer? What if you save more innocent lives, like you did for Canterbury? What if we end up having an incredible life together? I can't say your fears aren't justified, but they aren't everything. And for what it's worth, I think you'll be a great seer."

I sniffed. "Thanks."

"Hey, why don't you come see me? I want to show you something. Azalea can pick you up."

I took a deep, shaky breath. "I'm not sure I'm up for a house full of people," I admitted.

"Neither am I," he replied. "So it's a good thing I'm at the conservatory. Tell the people at the front desk that you're here for me, and they'll give you a pass. Once you get in, give me a call."

Why isn't he in bed?

"How did you know to call?"

"I just had a feeling you needed me," he replied.

"Are you sure *you* aren't the seer?"

He chuckled. "I don't think it would have worked for anyone else."

Azalea arrived a few minutes later in Lucas' truck, and Chrys and I climbed in. She looked upset and annoyed.

"Sorry," I instinctively apologized. I couldn't imagine she enjoyed playing chauffeur to her brother's girlfriend.

"What? No. This," she said as she gestured to her face, "isn't because of you. It's because of my idiot brother."

"Jonas? What did he do?"

Azalea laughed. "Three days! Three days, and you already have him pegged as the idiot brother. I'm gonna have to tell him. This is awesome! But no, this time, the idiot brother is the other one. Maybe you can talk some sense into him."

"Lucas? Is this because he's at the conservatory instead of home, resting?"

"Yep. The man doesn't know when to stop working."

Chapter 40

Lucas

I FELT LIKE I HAD A MILD SUNBURN ALL OVER MY BODY. It was uncomfortable and slightly painful, and everything hurt, but it was still a vast improvement over the previous few days. We dropped Miriam off, and I felt her absence like a missing limb. I wanted to call her and beg her to come back, but she needed space as much as I needed rest.

Canterbury sent me an image of the spring where we'd bonded. The closer we got to my house and the conservatory, the more I felt the need to go there.

"Dad, would you mind dropping me off at the conservatory instead of at home?"

His brows furrowed in concern. "Son, don't you think you should be resting?"

"Yeah, I will. I just … I think my base of power is there, and I need to spend some time in it."

Canterbury chirped.

"Little guy agrees with you. Very well, but keep your phone on you. Listen to your familiar. Always had more sense than any of my children."

I should have been offended by that, but that would have taken too much energy.

"Thanks, Dad."

"Promise you'll take it easy," Mom said.

I promised, and Mom left it at that, though I could tell she didn't like it. Dad pulled up to the conservatory doors, and I hobbled out of the car, Canterbury perched on my shoulder. I didn't have my badge with me, so I headed to the front desk, hoping whoever was on shift recognized me.

"Yo! Prof! You look like something the cat dragged in," Ollie, one of my students, greeted me from the front desk. "We heard you were in the hospital. Everything good?"

"Better than it was," I replied truthfully.

"The whole class missed you. Some of the students—mostly the girls—set up this chat dedicated to figuring out which hospital you were in so they could visit. Get any surprise visitors?"

No, thank heavens.

"No, just my family and girlfriend."

His eyes grew wide. "Girlfriend? Prof, where have you been hiding her? Oooh, half the class will be so heartbroken when they hear you're taken."

I grunted. I sincerely doubted that.

I waved at Ollie and shuffled past him and through the doors to the conservatory. I stepped back outside, and it felt like all of the plants turned their attention towards me. I froze—it was intimidating, feeling like nature was scrutinizing you and finding you lacking.

At Canterbury's urging, I continued on down the well-known paths I could walk in my sleep. Past the *Buddleja davidii*[8], the *Alcea rosea*[9], the *Hibiscus syriacus*[10], and the *Syringa vulgaris*[11]. Some of these wouldn't ordinarily survive in Arizona, but thanks to the magic springs and micro-climates they created, all manner of plants could thrive here.

I turned off the path through the Butterfly Garden and down the right-hand path lined with *Populus magicus*[12]. If anything, the trees felt more judgmental than the bushes had. I did my best to ignore them as I shuffled on.

Eventually, I arrived at the Little Whispering Spring Garden and collapsed onto the cool grass around it. Canterbury perched on my chest, and I felt the magic of the garden gather at the edge of my senses. It paused there as if waiting for something.

"I'm sorry," I whispered. "I'm trying to protect her, but I don't always know what's best. I messed up, and because of that, her kidnapper got away."

That seemed to appease the magic because it began to flow into me, gently, slowly, soothing the pain away. I relaxed with a deep, contented sigh. I was still exhausted, but the pain was ebbing. I lay there for several minutes before an uneasy feeling crept over me. Without thinking, I pulled my phone out of my

---

[8] *Buddleja davidii*: Butterfly bush
[9] *Alcea rosea*: Hollyhock
[10] *Hibiscus syriacus*: Rose of Sharon
[11] *Syringa vulgaris*: French Lilac
[12] *Populus magicus*: Magic Aspen. Has many fire-retardant and magic-amplifying properties.

pocket and dialed.

"Hello?"

"Miriam! Are you okay?"

She wasn't, and I knew that like I knew my own name, but I also knew that she wasn't in physical danger, not at the moment, anyway.

She cried into the phone, spilling all of her worries and concerns. My heart ached for her. I knew exactly how she felt because those were things I worried about too. I worried that I wouldn't be good enough and that she would end up hurt. But I also knew that I couldn't *not* try.

"What if?" I said. "What if you end up being an incredible seer? What if you save more innocent lives, like you did for Canterbury? What if we end up having an incredible life together? I can't say your fears aren't justified, but they aren't everything. And for what it's worth, I think you'll be a great seer."

I didn't just *think* it, I *knew* it. Hopefully one day, she'd know it too.

"Thanks."

I could hear the tears in her voice, and I wanted nothing more than to pull her into my arms and hold her until they stopped.

"Hey, why don't you come see me? I want to show you something. Azalea can pick you up."

I couldn't explain why, but I knew she needed to come. I also knew that if I left to go get her, I'd undo all the progress I'd made, and she'd have to haul my sorry hide back here.

"I'm not sure I'm up for a house full of people," she said quietly, her voice unsteady.

I felt that. My home, my normally quiet haven, was brimming with people. My family and friends were great, but all of them at once could be taxing on an introverted soul.

"Neither am I. So it's a good thing I'm at the conservatory. Tell the people at the front desk that you're here for me, and they'll give you a pass. Once you get in, give me a call."

"How did you know to call?"

"I just had a feeling you needed me."

"Are you sure *you* aren't the seer?" she joked.

"I don't think it would have worked for anyone else."

We hung up, and I closed my eyes as a heavy sense of foreboding washed over me. As long as Jason was still out there, Miriam wouldn't be safe. Sooner or later, things would come to a head, and I would need to be ready.

I picked up the phone again to make a couple more calls. Azalea wasn't happy that I wasn't home resting, and Ollie was excited that he was going to get to meet Miriam.

"No, Ollie, *please* do not ask her for a picture," I pleaded.

"But if I don't get one, no one will believe I actually met the Prof's elusive girlfriend."

"Ollie …"

"Yeah, yeah, I know. Privacy, professionalism, blah, blah, blah. You're in the Whispering Spring Garden, right?"

"Little Whispering Spring Garden," I corrected.

"Ah, right, okay. I'll go ahead and mark the path on the map for her."

"Thanks, Ollie. And don't forget to study for the quiz on Friday."

"Ah, man, Prof. Are we still doing that?"

"Yes, Ollie, we're still doing that."

Chapter 41

Miriam

WE ARRIVED AT THE CONSERVATORY a few minutes later, and I hopped out of the truck, Chrys' bowl clutched to my chest. Being a business day, there were several other cars in the parking lot, and I wondered how a crowd of strangers was better than a crowded house.

"Call me when you've beaten some sense into my brother," Azalea said before I closed the door.

I nodded.

There was a line of people at the front desk waiting to buy tickets. I quietly stood in line, waiting my turn. I was behind a small family with a young boy with an overabundance of energy.

"What's in your bowl?" he asked me, standing on his toes to get a better look. "Is it cereal? I had cereal for breakfast. I love cereal. But Mom says we can't bring food in here, so you should eat it before they kick you out. Do you know elephants are my favorite animal? They have long trunks and go *ppuuuooooeeerruuu!*"

That is the oddest elephant noise I have ever heard.

"Yeah, elephants are pretty cool, aren't they?"

"Gabe, love, what did we say about making elephant noises inside?"

"But Moooom, I needed to teach her what elephants sound like. She didn't know!"

"Did you ask if she knew what elephants sounded like?"

"No, but she didn't know! She didn't!"

His mom sighed. "I understand you were trying to help, just please remember to use your inside voice, okay? Elephant noises are *outside* noises."

"But—"

"Yes, Mom," his dad interrupted, giving him *the look.*

"Yes, Mom," Gabe pouted. He looked back at me. "Are you going to eat your cereal?"

My 'cereal' poked her head over the side of her bowl and chirped.

"Mom! Mom! Mom! Look! She's got a little bird in a bowl! It's so pretty! I want a bird in a bowl! Pleeeease! Can I have one?"

His mom sighed again. "Yes, that is a really cool bird, isn't it? But what have we talked about? Just because somebody else has something we like …"

"Doesn't mean we need it too," Gabe finished glumly.

"Sorry," his mom mouthed to me.

"It's fine," I said, "but she's not really a bird." I knelt down so Gabe could get a better look.

"It's a little griffin! I want to hold her!" He reached out, but his mom stopped him gently.

"Remember, bud, we look with our eyes, not our hands."

He nodded, then did a little happy dance. "She's soooo cuuute!"

I looked at Gabe and a funny feeling stole over me. "Hey, don't stand on the turtle's head. It will break."

Gabe snickered. "Silly, turtles aren't for riding."

"Alright! We've got our tickets! Who's ready for some plants?" his dad asked, gesturing dramatically to the conservatory entrance.

"Meeeee! Whoooo!" Gabe shouted, bolting for the door with his parents hot on his heels.

"Walking feet, Gabe! Walking feet!" his mom yelled.

I glanced down at Chrys. "Was that a ...?"

Chrys chirped in affirmation.

A prediction without a vision—this was getting complicated. *And what turtle?*

"You must be Miriam," the clerk said with a grin as I stepped up to the desk. "Lucas told us to expect you."

"Uh, yeah, how did you ..." I trailed off.

"Partly the poetic description of you, but mostly the teacup griffin," he said, nodding at Chrys.

Poetic description? Just what did Lucas say about me?

"Yeah, Chrys is pretty distinctive," I said as I took the ticket he handed me.

"Oh, here, you'll want this too," he said as he thrust a map at me. "Prof is at the Little Whispering Spring Garden. It can be a bit difficult to find, so I went ahead and marked the path for you."

"Thanks," I said with sincere appreciation.

I stepped through the lobby exit into the conservatory outside. I slid my ticket into my pocket and looked around in amazement. I'd always wanted to visit the conservatory Wellspring was famous for. I could hardly believe I was here, and for free! The magical springs here created micro-climates that allowed species of plants to thrive here that simply did not belong in the Arizona desert. I'd heard there was everything from a jungle clime to an arctic tundra.

I wanted to take time to explore everything, but Lucas was waiting for me, and I felt the need to hurry to him.

I started down the gravel path, amazed at the variety of flora I saw. I bet Lucas could name every single one and probably give a lecture on each of them. Butterflies and hummingbirds flitted from bush to bush, and the temperature dropped a few degrees. Chrys cheeped at me, and I held her up to a flowering shrub she seemed interested in.

Following the path the clerk marked for me, I turned left onto a tree-lined trail. A sense of déjà vu skittered down my spine, and I froze.

"There she is!" a voice shouted.

I turned, but all I could make out of the person was an indistinct, vaguely humanoid shape. My heart plummeted to my toes as more shapes joined the first.

Chrys shrieked, but I didn't need her warning. I turned and

sprinted down the path, knowing with absolute certainty that I needed to reach Lucas.

The gravel crunched loudly under my feet but wasn't enough to drown out the sound of my pursuers. I didn't need to look back to know they were gaining on me. I ran and ran, my lungs protesting, but I didn't dare stop.

I tripped over a root in the path but caught myself before face-planting. A quick glance over my shoulder showed my pursuers were closer, but their features were still indistinct, as if something was artificially blurring them.

I continued running.

"Lucas!" I shouted with what little breath I could spare.

A shadow blotted out the sun as a griffin landed in front of me. I skidded to a halt, stuck between the devil I knew and the devils I didn't.

The griffin shifted back, drawing a gun in a fluid motion.

"Get to Lucas!" he shouted. Then, more quietly, "I'm not the enemy here."

Just like my vision.

I darted around Agent Stone as the first shot rang out. I flinched, but it wasn't my scream that rent the air. I managed a few more steps before the ground shook. I nearly fell, but a net of vines and branches caught me, cradling me safely.

I looked back at my pursuers and gaped at the chaos that greeted me. It was as if nature had exploded and turned against them with vengeance. Each one was wrapped in thorny brambles, and I wouldn't have been surprised if several were bleeding—some of those thorns were as long as my hand.

Three of the trees grew, fusing together to form one massive tree. The trunk swelled, then split, and Lucas stepped out of it. His glowing eyes were filled with fury, and magic radiated from him. Canterbury stood on his shoulder, his own eyes glowing with shared magic.

"No one touches my seer," Lucas said, his voice echoing with power. "She is mine to protect."

A shiver zipped down my spine. His words were more than a simple declaration. There was magic in them, a binding vow. Lucas would protect me until his final breath.

He spun and raised his hand. Vines shot out, wrapping themselves around a griffin that had been trying to dive-bomb him. The vines pulled the griffin down, and he landed with a sickening crunch. Nothing moved after that.

More griffins?

I thought about my visions and everything Agent Stone had said to me.

Whump. Whump.

I looked up to find a red dragon circling overhead. I glanced at Lucas, afraid. A griffin wasn't much of a threat to him. But a fire-breathing dragon? Lucas, however, simply looked annoyed.

The dragon tucked its wings and dove, shifting a few feet from the ground. He landed on his feet and looked around with a huge grin. A distant part of my brain noted that he kept his clothes during his shift, which I thought was supposed to be impossible.

"I've always wanted to see a guardian in action. Impressive

work," Dylan said as he prodded the brambles around one of the attackers. "Did you really walk out of that tree?"

"Are you going to arrest these jokers, or do I need to turn them into fertilizer?"

"You are within your right as a guardian to do with them as you see fit. However, I think we'll get more information from them if we take them in. Mind holding them here until I get transport ready?"

Lucas shrugged. "You'll want a couple ambulances too. My brambles were none too gentle with them."

Chapter 42

Lucas

THE MAGIC COURSING THROUGH ME SLOWED from a mighty river to a burbling creek, and I breathed a sigh of relief. Channeling that much magic made my body feel like it was going to vibrate apart. Combined with the lingering sensation of being compressed as I traveled through the root system of the *Populus magicus,* I was left feeling weird. I would not be trying that again any time soon. I wouldn't have even attempted it this time if it hadn't been such an emergency.

I'd felt Miriam's fear as keenly as if it had been my own and acted instinctively. Thankfully, the magic of the land was more than willing to help me protect her. When I'd made my vow, the magic in me had redoubled, and I still felt echoes of its power in my chest.

"Yeah, we'll definitely need a couple ambulances," Dylan said, looking at the captives. He raised an eyebrow at Jason. "Don't think you'll be lucky enough to get away again."

Jason's face was pale and pinched in pain.

"Wait," Miriam said as she climbed out of the nest I'd made her. "He's not our enemy."

Of all the words I thought she would say, those were the last I'd expected. She walked over to me and took my hand while looking at Jason.

"You kidnapped me to keep me away from them, didn't you?" she asked, jerking her head at the other captive griffins.

"I thought it was my place to protect you, and it was my fault you were in danger."

I pulled Miriam closer, as if proximity to me was enough to protect her from what Jason was going to say next.

"When I told my father my suspicions about you being a seer, he believed that *I* would be your guardian. He convinced me to try to get close to you so I would be better positioned to take on the role."

Miriam scowled and wrinkled her nose. "That's what all that awful flirting was about? I suppose that explains a lot."

Jason let out a pained laugh. "Can't say my flirting abilities have ever been insulted before, but I can't say you're wrong either. Anyways, one day, when I was reporting on the … situation … a spy for the Shadow Clan overheard. They would do anything to control a seer. When we realized the information had leaked, Father ordered me to get Miriam and bring her back to our clan house."

I narrowed my eyes at him—his story didn't add up. "But your clan house was in the *other* direction."

"Being under my father's thumb wasn't a better solution. A gilded cage is still a cage."

"You planned to run away with me and stay in hiding the rest of our lives," Miriam said softly.

"Living free, but in hiding is better than living as someone's puppet."

I scowled, not buying his story. "But she wasn't free. You had her bound and gagged! She was crying, and hurt, and scared *because of you.* You weren't her savior—you were just another captor."

"I know," he said quietly. "I told myself I was doing the right thing, that there hadn't been time to explain the situation, that I would explain everything once we were safe. I ... I was wrong."

Just because he apologized didn't mean I needed to forgive him. Miriam, however, had a different opinion.

"You need to let him go," she said as she looked at me, her brown eyes luminous. "He's needed elsewhere."

The words were prophetic—a seer was speaking to me. But I still didn't want to.

She reached up and cupped my cheek in her hand. "He's no threat to me. Not anymore, not when I have you. It's safe to let him go."

I sighed and closed my eyes as I leaned into her touch. "Fine. But if he hurts you again, I'll kill him."

I glanced at Dylan.

He shrugged. "If it means one of my best friends, a man I looked up to, is a misguided idiot, and *not* evil, I'm okay with this. And if he hurts Miriam, I'll help you bury the body."

"With friends like these," Jason muttered, and I glared at him. "Yeah, I suppose I deserve it." He looked into my eyes. "I swear on my life that I will not harm the seer, Miriam, ever again."

He should never have harmed her in the first place, but it would have to do. I glanced at Miriam for confirmation again. When she nodded, I reached out with my magic and coaxed the brambles away from Jason. There was a little resistance, but nothing like it had been in the cave.

Jason's clothing was torn and bloodied, but he didn't stick around to get checked out. He shifted into his griffin form and took off. Dylan watched him leave, a pained expression on his face.

"He's still a fugitive, you know. There's still a warrant out for his arrest. He can't just go back like nothing happened."

"I know," Miriam said quietly. "But he belongs elsewhere now. His old life doesn't fit him anymore. You'll need to get those warrants dropped … eventually."

I could hear the sirens growing closer. In what felt like no time at all after that, the place was swarming with law enforcement and paramedics. Even Dylan's SAID team made an appearance.

Miriam and I were questioned over and over again. It got to the point where I considered dragging everyone into a classroom and giving a presentation so they could all hear it at once.

Chapter 43

Miriam

"That was exhausting," I said when the police finally shooed us out of their crime scene.

"It was," Lucas agreed as he led me away.

I expected him to head back to the entrance, but instead, he led me deeper into the conservatory.

"Where are we going?"

"You still haven't seen what I wanted to show you," he said.

Part of me wanted to protest, but the other part of me still desperately wanted to see more of this magical place.

We strolled hand-in-hand down the picturesque paths, and I was seized with the desire to pull this man into a shadowy alcove and kiss him silly. I was on the lookout for just such a place when he suddenly stopped.

"We're here," he announced.

I felt a flash of disappointment that my alcove-hunting had to be put on pause, but then I saw it. We'd stopped by a quietly burbling spring bordered by pretty rocks and surrounded by the softest grass I had ever seen. Grass like this was an impossibility in Arizona. The spring called to me like an old friend. I'd never been here before, but deep down, my soul knew this place.

As if in a trance, I walked over to the spring and gazed into the water. In the bowl, Chrys chirped. The water glowed as a ripple spread out from the center of my gaze. It stilled, and a picture formed in it, clear as day.

A troll sat at a table, scarfing down a bowl of peanuts by the handful. He muttered something unintelligible as he ate. His face grew blotchy and began to swell. His breathing grew coarse and ragged. He looked up, a concerned and confused expression on his face. He reached for his phone and dialed 9-1-1, but by the time the operator answered, he had already slumped over the table, unconscious. Help would not arrive in time.

"Geeze! Is there a way to change the setting on this? I want happy visions!"

"What did you see?" Lucas asked in alarm.

"A troll dying of anaphylaxis. He looked familiar, but I can't place him."

Lucas grimaced. "Maybe you'll meet him soon and can warn him of it?"

"Maybe," I agreed glumly. "I'd still rather happy visions."

"Understandable," he replied.

"So, this is it then? This spring is my focus? What … what do I do with this information? Where do I go from here? I can't just stay here all the time having visions—that sounds like an awful life. I also can't afford to buy a ticket every time I want to come here for a vision. And what about my job?"

"Hey," Lucas said as he slipped his arms around me, "none of these questions need to be answered right now. And I promise no one's going to chain you to the spring and make you keep having visions. No one will make you do anything you don't want to do. They'll have to deal with me first. As for the tickets, I can get you a guest pass if needed. But something tells me it's illegal to charge a seer to use their focus."

I sniffed. "Sorry. I'm probably being a bit crazy about this."

Lucas held me close. "No, you're not. This is a big deal, and there's a lot to think about, and a lot of things are going to change, but not everything needs to happen at once. We can take our time—trees don't grow in a day."

"Unless you have anything to say about that."

He laughed. "I suppose. But slow and steady is more sustainable."

"This doesn't feel slow and steady. It feels like a whirlwind picked me up and hasn't put me down yet."

"I know. Let's just sit for a few minutes. Don't worry about anyone or anything else for a bit. Just sit and exist."

I followed his lead and lay down on the soft grass. I rested my head on his shoulder and snuggled in. It wasn't kissing him silly in an alcove, but it was a close second. I closed my eyes and tried to relax. Lying there with Lucas, it was easy to let go of my worries, fears, and anxiety. I snuggled in close and threw an arm around him. He gently stroked my back in silence.

"OMG, you two are just the cutest!" a voice said.

I begrudgingly opened my eyes to find the front desk clerk beaming down at us.

"Ollie, I swear, I'm going to assign you a fifty-page report on the relationship between soil acidity and the quality of fruit from the *Fragaria magicus*[13] if you don't go away."

"Aww! No fair! I was just coming to check on you after the recent hubbub. They closed down the conservatory for the day, but neither of you came out. I was worried you were one of the ones taken in the ambulance. I mean, none of them *looked* like you two, but I wasn't certain. Did you know someone made an absolute mess of Magic Tree Way? It's going to take *ages* to get it fixed. Someone even broke the head off the turtle statue. We had police and SAID agents swarming this place, and you're just here canoodling with your girlfriend."

"Goodbye, Ollie," Lucas said, his eyes still closed.

Ollie yelped as a vine wrapped around him and carted him away.

"Hmm … do you think that would be considered an abuse of power?" Lucas asked.

"We'll say you were protecting my peace," I replied, closing my eyes again.

"I like the way you think."

We lay like that for several more minutes before another unwelcome but less easily removed interruption ended our peace.

"I just had an irate employee talk my ear off about his 'ungrateful professor' who used magic and vines to throw him out 'like yesterday's garbage.' You wouldn't happen to know what he's talking about, would you?" Dylan asked, looking

---

[13] *Fragaria magicus:* species of magical blueberries.

down at us with an amused expression.

"Nope. Doesn't sound familiar," Lucas replied. "I've just been here with my girlfriend, minding my own business."

"Riiiight. I also got a text from your mom saying that I was to bring you back home, willingly or otherwise. She promised me a giant steak, so are you going to walk, or do I have to carry you?"

Lucas sighed wearily. "Fine. We're coming."

"Miriam, Lucas' mom says you are more than welcome to come, but I'm not to force you to do anything you don't want to do, but if I do manage to convince you, I get a second steak. So ..."

I laughed. "I guess you get two steaks, then."

"Score! Lucas, your girlfriend's the best."

"I know."

Chapter 44

Miriam

LUCAS' HOUSE WAS A MESS. The floor in the living room had been ripped up, and most of the furniture was missing. A few folding tables and several chairs stood as temporary replacements for the sofa and coffee table.

"I … forgot about this," Lucas said, eying the damage.

"What … what happened?" I asked.

"Lucas happened," Dylan replied, giving his friend a solid thump on the back. "Let's just say he wasn't handling your kidnapping very well."

"I see …"

"Miriam, dear, thank you so much for joining us," Hester said, giving me a hug. "Go sit. Let me whip up something for you real quick."

I smiled and thanked her, knowing better than to refuse her offer. In gnomish culture, that offer was an expression of love.

"And I haven't forgotten your steaks, Dylan. How do you like them?"

"Rare, please."

"Of course, dear."

"I'm beginning to feel like an afterthought," Lucas muttered.

Hester pegged him with a look. "You'll get whatever I make your girlfriend, you stubborn man. You're going to sit and eat, and then you're going to bed to get some rest. I'd say I don't know where you get it from, but I'm pretty sure it's your father."

"Yes, ma'am," Lucas said with a grin.

"Lucas!" Nolan shouted, appearing suddenly behind Hester, which was a feat considering how much taller he was. He stepped around Hester and grabbed Lucas' shoulders. "We heard sirens and saw ambulances, but Dylan wouldn't tell us anything. Are you okay?"

"Yeah, I'm fine," Lucas replied.

"He saved me and foiled a kidnapping attempt," I added. "He was incredible."

Dylan shrugged. "He was alright, if you like people glowing with magic, turning trees into portals, throwing around bad guys like they're rag dolls, and rescuing damsels in distress."

I looked at Dylan. "Didn't you come *after* most of that, though?"

"The security cameras had top-notch footage. It was like watching a movie. Almost asked where the popcorn was. Sadly, some of the footage at the end was corrupted, probably from a magical surge."

I nodded at him—he'd get in a lot of trouble for that if anyone found out, but I had a feeling it would all turn out fine in the end.

We sat at the table where a familiar troll also sat, chowing down on a peanut butter sandwich. I lunged across the table and smacked the sandwich out of his hands. He, and everyone else, stared at me in shock.

I looked at the troll. "No peanuts for you. Ever. Period. They. Will. Kill. You."

Lucas' mom quickly scooped up the half-eaten sandwich and disposed of it.

The troll scowled at us. "That's bunk. You can't just come in here and take my spicy lil nuts away." His voice was thick, and he gasped for breath as he spoke.

Nolan snickered.

"Brick, do you think peanuts are spicy?" Dylan asked.

"Yeah, man, I love those spicy little pieces of joy, especially smeared on a sandwich with sweet jelly."

"Do you ever have trouble breathing after you have peanuts and peanut butter?" a man I didn't know asked.

"Sometimes, but only because I eat too fast," he said.

Nolan sobered up immediately. "Dude," he said, "I shouldn't have laughed. You're allergic to peanuts."

The troll scoffed. "No, I'm not."

"Yeah, dude, you are," Nolan said. "Nobody else has trouble breathing after eating peanuts, no matter how fast they eat them."

"And no one else thinks they're spicy either," Dylan added.

"Before we got here, Miriam had a vision of a troll—you—

dying of anaphylaxis," Lucas said.

"Oh." Brick looked abashed. "Sorry, Miss Seer. Er, thanks for saving my life. I won't eat peanuts."

"It's fine. Sorry for smacking your sandwich. I kind of panicked."

"Here, Brick, try this," Hester said, putting a plate in front of the troll. "It's spicy tahini with strawberry jam. I'm not sure how spicy you like things, so I only added a little bit of chili paste. If you want it spicier, I can add more."

Brick glanced at me, and I shrugged.

"I only know about the peanuts," I said, grateful that my terrible vision wasn't likely to come to pass now.

Maybe ... maybe if I can stop bad things from happening it will be worth it.

He picked up the slice of bread and took a tentative bite, chewed, swallowed, then shoved the rest of it in his mouth.

"That was delicious Mrs. Fernleaf."

With that declaration, an invisible weight lifted off the group, and we all relaxed. Hester had the rest of our food out in short order. Lucas and I had turkey and cranberry croissant sandwiches while Dylan scarfed down two steaks.

"Thank you, that was delicious," I said to Hester.

"Of course, dear, anytime."

Lucas yawned, which prompted me to yawn.

"Alright you two, off to bed. You've had a long day."

Before I realized what was happening, we were tucked into bed and dozing off. My last coherent thought was that this was infinitely better than the hospital bed.

Tesha Geddes

Chapter 45

Lucas

I HAD TO HAND IT TO MY MOM—SHE WAS A GENIUS. I'd been awake for several minutes already, but Miriam was still asleep, pressed close against my side. On the dresser, Chrys and Canterbury slept together in Chrys' bowl. The smells wafting under my door had my mouth watering, but it would take more than even my mother's cooking to get me to move.

Miriam stirred and stretched. "Mmmm … is that bacon?"

"Probably."

"Jonas is going to eat it all if we don't hurry, isn't he?"

"Probably."

"Is that the only word you know this morning?"

"Probably."

She gave me a playful shove. "Just for that, see if I leave you any bacon."

"You don't pull any punches, do you?"

She gave me a kiss before vaulting out of bed, saying, "All's fair in love and bacon."

"That's not how that saying goes!" I protested as I chased after her.

Chrys and Canterbury chirped, cheering Miriam on.

"Traitor!" I shouted at my familiar.

He laughed at me.

"You two are looking better this morning," Mom greeted us as we entered the kitchen. She was manning the griddle while Jonas cooked bacon, and my other siblings sat at the table chopping various fruits and vegetables.

My friends had all left at some point while I was at the hospital, allowing my family to stay in my guest rooms, though Jonas was relegated to the couch, and my sisters were crammed into one room together, with two on the bed and one on an air mattress. I felt bad that anyone had to stay here while my house was in such disarray.

"I've got crepes this morning. Are you feeling sweet or savory?" Mom asked.

My stomach rumbled. "One of each?"

Mom beamed at me, and I couldn't help but feel like I'd passed some sort of test. Maybe the Lucas-is-feeling-better test. Miriam placed her crepe order, and soon, we were all sitting around the table enjoying a family breakfast. I couldn't speak for my family, but it felt like Miriam belonged there, a piece we never knew was missing.

I was just polishing off my second crepe when the door opened, and Dylan waltzed in. He walked into the kitchen and promptly helped himself to a crepe, piling it high with eggs, bacon, sausage, and cheese. By the time he was done, it more resembled a breakfast taco than a crepe. There was no more room around the table, so he leaned against the counter while he ate. I mentally shrugged. Dylan would tell us why he was here eventually. In the meantime, he was welcome to food—he would always be welcome to food here.

"So, I take it none of you have watched the news yet this morning," he said after he polished off his third crepe taco.

I froze, my glass of water halfway to my mouth. I instinctively reached for Miriam's hand as I set the glass down. "What's on the news?"

"Speculations about a new seer," he replied. He looked at Miriam apologetically. "I'm sorry. I tried to keep it under wraps as best as I could, but someone spilled the beans to a major news channel."

She sighed. "It was bound to happen sooner or later. I would have preferred later, but," she squeezed my hand, "we'll make the best of it. I take it you're going to be my official SAID liaison now? Part bodyguard, part whatever."

"Sure, ruin the surprise," Dylan grumbled. "Dang seers."

I bristled. Did the government really think I was such a poor guardian that they sent someone else to protect Miriam?

"It's not like that, Lucas," Dylan said, correctly guessing my thoughts. "While I will function as a sort of backup bodyguard, my main job will be to run point between Miriam and other government agencies. It will be my responsibility to report any significant visions she has as well as pass on vision requests they might have. Before you panic about getting inundated with requests, there are strict guidelines about what the government can ask a seer to look into. Typically along the lines of natural disasters, helping with significant crimes, etc. They can only submit one request per situation, so you don't have to worry about being inundated with requests for the same thing. And, of course, since you'll be working for the government, you'll get a nice salary. I saw the numbers—seers get paid well." He nodded at me. "And so do their guardians."

"Excuse me," Miriam said, pushing her chair back with a loud scraping sound, "I need a minute."

She hurried out the back door as I glared at Dylan. There had to have been a better way to present the information. I quietly excused myself and hurried after my girlfriend.

I found her sitting on the bench in my cactus garden, hugging herself. I sat down next to her and pulled her into my arms. She turned and buried her face in my chest. I could feel her heart racing as she shook.

"I'm sorry. I don't know why I'm … I'm sorry. I'll be fine. I just feel like … like …"

"Like it's happening too fast? Like your life is spiraling out of control? Like suddenly you're not the one in charge anymore?"

She nodded.

"You don't have to do this. If you want to run away and not be a seer, I'll pack your bag. If you want to stay but tell the government to take a hike, I'll buy a walking stick and beat them with it. If you want to stay and give the seer thing a shot, I'll stand by you and support you any way I can."

She took a deep breath and squeezed me tightly before looking up at me. "Thank you, Lucas. I know this has thrown your life into as much disarray as mine, and I'm probably selfish for saying this, but I'm glad that it was you."

"That's my line," I said before kissing her.

She tasted like strawberry crepes.

"And here I thought something was wrong," a voice drawled. "I should have known you two just snuck off for some face time."

I glared at my friend. "If you're going to stick around, you've got to stop interrupting."

"Or you could just stop kissing in public," Dylan pointed out.

Well, that's not happening. One look at Miriam told me she felt the same way.

Tesha Geddes

Epilogue

Miriam

I FINISHED RECORDING MY LAST VISION AND STRETCHED. I closed the laptop with a satisfying *click* and pushed my chair away from my desk. The visions today hadn't been bad, a little boring, but nothing horrific. I preferred it this way.

Chrys fluttered in through the open window and landed on my shoulder. I stroked her head all the way down to her fluffy little tail, and she arched her back in delight.

It had taken me a few weeks to find my stride as a seer, and Chrys played a vital role in helping me channel the magic for my visions so they didn't completely overtake me. Most of the time, I had to ask the spring to show me a vision, but sometimes, one would sweep over me when I was away from it.

Now that she was healed and off her medication (and I was off mine), Chrys was able to give me ample warning before a vision so I could sit down. Learning that watching a vision in the spring water was easier on me, physically and mentally, Lucas fashioned a pendant for me. It was a simple, miniature glass sphere that he filled with spring water and hung on a chain with a chrysocolla bead and some pearls. I joked that he made me the world's smallest crystal ball. He just laughed and said I wasn't wrong. It worked, though—it worked so well, he made a few extra and even carried one around himself, just in case mine broke and I needed an emergency replacement.

Every time I had a vision away from the spring, I was able to focus it through the pendant and not lose myself completely. Thanks to Chrys' warnings, and Lucas' ingenuity, I hadn't had a seizure-vision in weeks. I hadn't realized how much stress they had caused me until they were gone. Taking a minute to sit and stare at a piece of jewelry was a vast improvement.

I took a moment to tidy up the small office and close and latch the window before I left. With the university's permission, Lucas had built—grown—me a cottage out of a species of magical tree beside the spring, which had been re-dubbed The Seer's Spring. It was a small one-room cottage, and while it was beautiful and suited all my office needs, I was grateful I didn't have to live here.

The spring and surrounding area had been fenced off, and Lucas had grown a privacy hedge around the entire thing, leaving only two gated entrances. The gates were short and could easily be climbed over, but their mere presence kept most people out.

I stepped out the door right into Lucas' waiting arms.

"Excellent timing, as always," I said before kissing him.

He grinned. "A little birdie told me you were getting ready to leave."

"Tattle-tale," I teased as I stroked Canterbury's head.

"Ready for our date tonight?" Lucas asked.

"Absolutely," I said and then kissed him again.

Across the spring, a pair of young teacup griffins flitted from flower to flower.

The End

Afterword

Pretend I wrote something hilarious here. Take a moment, chuckle to yourself. Remark on my wit.

Thank you!

Also, I would love it if you would take a moment to leave a rating or review.

About the Author

Has anyone ever mentioned that it's weird to talk about yourself in third person? Trust me, it is. I love books (obviously). I've always dreamed of being an author and I'm super excited and nervous to share with you the worlds my crazy imagination comes up with. I love to bake, and I spend lots of time looking up recipes, only to realize I don't have the ingredients and I'm too lazy to go to the store.

If you want to keep informed on upcoming books and whatever's going on, go to my Facebook page, Tesha Geddes Writes.

Other books by Tesha Geddes

The Pocket Dragon Series:
The Pocket Dragon (Book 1)
The Healer Dragon (Book 2)
The Rebel Dragon (Book 3)

Mysteries of Magic Series:
Magus Rising (Book 1)
Magus Revealed (Book 2)
Magus Chosen (Book 3)
Magus Tide (Book 4)

On Wings of Light Series:
The Phoenix Stone (Book 1)

Made in the USA
Las Vegas, NV
03 March 2025